THE HOUNDS OF HELL

by Ron Fortier
and Gordon Linzner

AIRSHIP 27 PRODUCTIONS

Published by Airship 27 Productions
www.airship27.com www.airship27hangar.com

Cover © 2008 Tom Floyd
Illustrations © 2008 Rob Davis & Bradley Walton
Production and design by Rob Davis
Original Hounds of Hell logo by Vincent Sneed

ISBN-13: 978-0692465141 (Airship 27)
ISBN-10: 0692465146

Third Editon

Printed in the United States of America

10 9 8 7 6 5 4 3 2 1

CONTENTS

THE HOUNDS OF HELL CHANGED MY LIFE

by Barry Reese

T he Hounds of Hell changed my life.

Sounds like hyperbole, doesn't it? It's not—I firmly believe that every writer has a handful of transformative works in their life. Ones that shape their destiny as a creator – and the story you're holding in your hands right now is one of those for me.

When I first discovered this book, it was 2006 and The Hounds of Hell had been in print for almost a year. I was plugging along doing work for Marvel Comics and West End Games but I was itching to do something that would be more "me" in terms of content. I was considering doing the do-it-yourself route on a novel so I started surfing around and looking at other small or independent publishers to see what could be done... and along the way I stumbled onto a small-press outfit that was publishing new stories told in the classic pulp style.

I was floored.

I had grown up on a steady diet of Doc Savage, The Shadow, John Carter and Conan. I thought that tales like that were a thing of the past – but here was something called The Hounds of Hell that certainly looked like it could have emerged from that same era.

I didn't hesitate very long before I ordered it and I began devouring every word when it finally arrived at my home. The pacing, the character development, the interior artwork... it all reminded me of the joyous days of my youth, when the prose could get my blood pumping. It reminded me of why I dreamed of becoming a writer – and it stirred something else within me: the realization that I didn't have to write The Great American Novel. I could write something fun. I could write the kinds of stories that I loved to read as a kid... and, to be honest, that I was still hungry for as an adult.

I read The Hounds of Hell twice before coming up with The Conquerors of Shadow. On the surface, the two books aren't all that similar – one is an homage to the classic hero pulps and the other is a planetary romance in the vein of Edgar Rice Burroughs – but I never would have had the bravery to write Conquerors without Hounds to lead the way. Suddenly I knew that pulp adventure could still survive in today's cynical world… and I wanted in.

After that, I created a few more New Pulp heroes: The Peregrine, Lazarus Gray, Gravedigger… more than a few, to be honest. I've been writing pulp for nearly ten years myself and I don't see an end in sight. What my writing career has become can all be traced back to my discovery of The Hounds of Hell. It told me that heroes and pulp adventure were not something to be left behind to the moldy old magazines and paperbacks of the past. We could add to that lore in the here-and-now.

If you're about to read this story for the first time, you're in an adrenaline-filled treat. If, like me, it's a revisiting of old friends, it's going to feel like going home.

Enjoy!

Barry Reese

May 2015

CHAPTER [1]
THE DARK ANGEL

Rain fell in torrents on the streets of Great City. Thousands of tiny wet pearls reflected the harsh glint of street lamps striving toward off the chill of night. Thoroughfares stretched cold and empty, seemingly aware of the dark evil latent in this miserable onslaught. They alone would bear witness to the horror which the storm augured.

A brilliant flash of lightning outlined a lone figure, one man racing through the downpour, splashing ankle-deep in curb side puddles. He was a comical balloon of humanity, barely five feet tall and very overweight. But there was no humor in his frantic haste, nor in the panic expressed by his pudgy face.

The runner's clothes were drenched clear through against the fearsome weather. One trouser knee was torn, showing he had fallen. A shirtsleeve was stained by blood.

The fugitive gulped great quantities of air. His hungry lungs also sucked in rainwater, gagging his throat. Raindrops dribbled into his eyes to blind him.

If only he could stop to rest, just for a minute! But the sodden racer dared not. Terror sped his heels. He lurched forward with renewed effort as new sounds reached his ears.

Bays and yelps echoed over the patter of rain on asphalt.

The dogs were loose!

In his fear, he tripped, gouging the other knee and rolling heavily into the gutter. Foul water clogged his mouth. He spluttered, spat the oily stuff out, scrambled once more to his feet.

A shadowed alleyway gaped before him; darkness promised sanctuary to his dread-filled mind. The murk of this urbanized grotto was tangible. It engulfed the runner in a deceptively protective blanket, though even within its borders he did not stop his frenzied rush.

An ominous padding broke the stillness of the commercial district. The dogs were drawing closer.

Now he stumbled over broke bottles and ill-smelling bags of garbage. Rats scurried before him, startled not so much by the intrusion of their scavenging grounds as by the sheer dread the man seemed to radiate. Something squished unpleasantly beneath his foot.

The fugitive paid no heed to these mundane discomforts. Death was at his heels. He sobbed aloud, in anguish, for a release from his torment.

Then, with a painful crash, he struck the rough brick wall at the end of his desperate path. Fate had played its final trick. He'd sought safety in a blind alley. There was no escape.

He spun around, back to the wall, to face the street. As last he could see the dogs. They padded across the rain-slicked blacktop with easy loping gaits, recklessly spattering brown water with their paws. In all, there were ten ruthlessly efficient Doberman and German Shepherds, each instructed to attack and kill without mercy. The man in the alley knew too well how hopeless was his plight. He was responsible for their sanguinary programming; he alone had trained these beasts.

The animals howled in savage triumph, sensing that their prey was trapped. The quarry was cornered, the death blow imminent.

Yet the dogs inexplicably drew up short at the mouth of the alley. They mingled in the rain, growling ominously at the fat man, but they came no closer. They appeared to be consciously prolonging his torture with an almost human gloating. It was a terrifying sight.

And then a second man appeared, coming up behind the dogs, and the hunted one shook with intensified fear.

The new player in the macabre drama wore a robe of deep scarlet which was bone-dry in spite of the downpour. He moved with a dancer's grace, stepping forward amidst the canine stalkers to peer into the closed passage's blackness.

His face was hidden by a cloth mask of a copper sheen, void of warmth and expression. Blood-red garments reached up to conceal the rest of his head, locking into a joining skull cap.

Two long, pointed horns protruded above the crest of his forehead.

A cold, inhuman laugh echoed form the devil-garbed figure. Icicles of fear knifed the entrapped man's heart.

"It ends here, then," followed a cruel voice.

"No!" the fat man begged. He crawled forward into the dim light, unable to stand in the face of such awesome terror. "Please! I wasn't going to the coppers! Don't kill me! Please!"

"It's too late for foolish lies. Your petty thoughts cannot elude Doctor Satan. Now you will suffer the fate of all who would betray me!"

The gruesome night hunter raised his hands above his head, looking for all the world like a great symphony conductor reaching a crescendo. But his was a symphony of death, and his instruments a pack of mindless, bloodthirsty brutes. At his signal, the dogs leapt into the alley.

In a desperate expression of his will to live, in the face of even such hopeless odds, the doomed man cuffed the first dog to reach him. The beast halted, stunned. For one brief fraction of a second, the trainer was once more in command.

Then they were all on him. Needle-sharp fangs ripped his flesh, shredding the rest of his clothing. The man screamed in agony, again and again, until one dog found his throat; then he screamed no more.

Doctor Satan watched the trainer's death agonies with reflective calm. When he was certain that the life was spent, he lowered his hands to bury them in the loose-flowing sleeves.

At that same moment the dogs quieted. They paid no further heed to the bloated carcass, waiting only on their new master's next order.

Satan glanced up at the evil clouds of gray. Rain streaked across his hideous mask; his coal-black eyes glowed with rapture between narrow slits.

Death's dark angel was content once more.

CHAPTER [2] A STRANGE TRANSFORMATION

"So this is what they mean by 'a dog's life'," sneered Detective Lieutenant Gilbert McEwen, head of the Great City Police Department's plainclothes division. This observation was made about the Sixth Annual Community Dog Show, spread across the lawn of the vast Gordon estate, and its participating pampered pooches.

The heavy rains had let up early that morning, leaving the afternoon crisp and cool and clear - perfect Autumn weather. Scores of well-dressed couples, the cream of Great City society, strolled among the gaily decorated canvas booths littering the well-manicured grounds. And everywhere were dogs of all shapes and sizes - toy poodles and Great

Danes, button-nosed terriers and dignified wolfhounds and comically ugly bulldogs - each one catered to, fussed over, waited hand and paw on by a doting owner.

"You can't blame the animals, Gil," replied the clean-cut young man standing at McEwen's side. Like the lieutenant, he wore a plain black suit; he, too, was here on police business.

Detective Sergeant Stephen Thatcher was the brightest young cop on the force, and his companion's future son-in-law to boot. "You have to give the owners their due," he added.

"Sure, sure," the ace sleuth growled back. "But it rankles me to see dumb mutts treated better than people. Half of these animal-lovers wouldn't give a dime for a cup of coffee to some poor Joe on a street corner."

"That's the rich for you, foot-loose and fancy free."

"That's another thing that gripes me, Steve. The show's entire take, in cash, is still on the grounds. It's a mighty tempting haul for a certain fancy crook I know."

"Come off it, Gil. You've got every entrance to the estate sealed off with uniformed men and half the undercover dicks in the department keeping an eye peeled on the patrons. I wouldn't be surprised to learn you'd dressed the other half in dog suits.

Do you still believe the Moon Man will make a play for that loot against those odds?"

"For twenty-two thousand in cash, I'll say he will. I've been on this bird's tail from the first, Steve. I know how he operates. He's got some angle doped out. I can almost smell him. I might as well tell you, I won't stop sweating until that money is downtown and in the vault of the Day and Night National."

Steve nodded, glancing at his wristwatch. "Well, you can rest easy soon," he said. "It's near the time for Mark and the guards to make the switch. I'd better get to my post."

"Check. I'll see to the armored car at the front gate. Keep a keen eye out, Steve!"

The lieutenant vanished into the milling crowd, on his way to supervise the final loading of the money sacks. Thatcher, according to orders, was to stake out the mansion's back entrance. But the clever young detective had different plans for the new few minutes.

Steve slipped quietly to the rear of the enormous white colonial structure and entered a garden maze formed out of tall, thick bushes. During that morning's preliminary survey of security precautions, he'd had ample time to discover how well this greenery suited his needs.

A narrow marble bench lay at the center of the maze. Seated on it was a burly, dark-faced man with cauliflower ears and no visible neck. His meaty hands clutched the grip of a bulging black leather case which rested on his lap.

The two exchanged brief smiles of recognition.

"Hurry, Angel," Steve urged. "We haven't much time."

"Right, boss!" came the snappy reply.

The huge man unlatched his burden, exposing its strange contents. Steve pulled a long black robe out of it. In a swift and practiced motion, he slipped it over his shoulders. The garment's hem just touched the top of the detective's shoes.

Next he withdrew and donned a pair of thin, ebon gloves. Lastly, with great care, he lifted out two fragile hemispheres of silvered glass. These he clasped together over his head, so the dark-cloaked shoulders seemed to support an opaque globe.

In a matter of seconds, Sergeant Steve Thatcher, defender of the law, ceased to exist. In his place stood the mysterious master criminal known only as the Moon Man.

"Gosh, boss!" cautioned the second man, former prize-fighter Ned 'Angel' Dargan. "Are you sure this is a smart move? McEwen's got this place sealed tighter than a drum. You've never pulled off a daylight caper before."

"We've already discussed this, Angel," replied the Moon Man.

The grotesque helmet distorted his voice past recognition. "I have to strike now! Once that money reaches the bank vault, it's out of my reach. I can't pass up the slimmest chance; too many people may suffer and die for want of that money!"

Dargan nodded silently. It was he, as the Moon Man's loyal ambassador, who distributed all their ill-gotten gains to the poor and needy. The fighter shared the moral code by which the Moon Man lived, a code that required the breaking of civil laws to obey nobler standards of decency. Channelled through bureaucratic red tape, less than a third of all monies collected for charity would reach those for whom it was intended if these two had not chosen to play modern-day equivalents of the legendary Robin Hood.

"Take the empty case back to the car, Angel," instructed the disguised Steve Thatcher. "Keep the motor running. If all goes well, I'll see you in five minutes."

"What if there's trouble?"

"Then beat it out of here, fast!"

"But, boss.."

"That's an order. You can't help me if we're both caught."

Again the fighter nodded, glumly. In the end, capture would lead the pair to the electric chair, for an unprovable false charge of murder hung over their heads. Both willingly accepted this risk. The lives of two men were as nothing, compared to the sufferings of impoverished thousands.

CHAPTER [3]
FANGS OF DEATH

At the main entrance of the Gordon mansion, huge oak doors of six inch thickness and nearly twice a man's height slowly swung open. Plush golden carpeting led from this portal into the opulent depths of the building, dividing into tributaries to climb the massive double staircase which half filled the entrance hall. Sunlight never touched this foyer to fade the elegant trappings, in spite of its southern exposure, for an elaborate Romanesque portico blocked such light at the top of the exterior marble steps.

Three stern-faced men stepped out of this modern palace. Two of them were in their late fifties, wearing brown and gray uniforms of the First Midwest armored car company. They bore a bulging gray moneybag apiece, and cradled deadly-looking shotguns.

Leading them, with his own weapon held at the ready in both hands, was Detective Lieutenant Mark Keanan, a man who bowed only to McEwen in his relentless pursuit of the Moon Man.

At this moment, the object of both lieutenants's enmity was studying the grim procession from the cover of tall shrubbery lining the twisting path to the main gate. Within the ball of Argus glass, sweat beaded on the Moon Man's forehead. He reached anxiously into the pocket of his cloak. The cool metal of his automatic pistol felt reassuring through the thin fabric of his ebon gloves.

His plan depended fully on the element of surprise. He had to come upon the trio so suddenly they would have no chance to use their guns. A million to one shot, but he had to run that risk.

Keanan's foot scraped at the smooth-paved path at the foot of the marble steps. The Moon Man tensed for action. In that fraction of a second before he made his play, all his senses were at their keenest. The background yelping of the show's dogs seemed to intensify.

Then chaos suddenly broke loose.

Half a dozen snarling German shepherds crashed through the shrubbery opposite the Moon Man's hiding place, leaping for the officials. Stunned by the savage, unexpected attack, all three men were knocked to the ground by the brutes. At such close quarters, the shotguns were worse than useless.

Under the charging weight of two dogs, one uniformed guard didn't have a chance to break his fall. His skull struck the marble step with a sickening crack, killing him instantly.

His companion was not so lucky. The gun flew from his hand at the impact of an animal's muzzle, landing several feet from his reach. He recovered quickly, scrambling to his knees, but he was surrounded by hungry, dripping fangs. He punched one beast on the jaw hard enough to loosen some teeth, but the razor-keen incisors of a second found his throat. Blood gushed in an unholy fountain. A horrible gurgle escaped the man's lips before he, too, was dead.

Keanan rolled with the attack, tumbling onto the soft grass at the path's edge. The cop's legs lashed out, kicking frantically at his own pair of canine assassins. One beast ripped open his pants at the thigh, removing a good piece of flesh along with the cloth. Keanan bit his tongue to stifle a scream of pain, redoubling his efforts to aim his weapon for a shot. All six dogs now turned their attention on the tenacious dick, closing in for the kill.

KAPOW!

A single gunshot shattered the air. The dog nearest Keanan's throat flipped into the air, with a gore-stained fragment of pants-cloth still clenched in its jaw. It was dead before it struck the ground.

Another shot rang out and a second dog caved to the earth, never to rise again.

The Moon Man stood at the lip of the path with a smoking automatic in his hand. Like Keanan and the others, the criminal had been shocked immobile while two men were brutally slain before his eyes. He would not watch a third death if he could prevent it.

His entry into the fray had an unanticipated consequence. The dogs abruptly ceased their bizarre attack, as if recognizing they were no match for an armed and wary adversary. Two of the surviving shepherds clamped powerful jaws on the money bags and carried them off into the greenery, fleeing as they'd come. The second pair followed close behind.

The Moon Man paused, trying to sort out that the last few seconds had wrought. Two armed guards were dead. Detective Keanan was seriously wounded. Somewhere a police whistle blew in response to the costumed figure's gunfire.

The last decided Thatcher's course of action. To remain meant certain capture. And the mystery dogs were escaping with over twenty grand in hard cash. If the Moon Man were ever to regain that money for his own worthy purpose, he had to follow them.

He stepped toward the break in the shrubbery made by the beasts. He did not do more than that. A stern, steel-hard voice, edged with pain, froze him in his tracks.

"Don't move, Moon Man, or you're dead!"

Despite his injury, Keanan pulled himself to a half-sitting position. He supported himself with his left arm. In his right hand was the shotgun he'd held onto throughout his desperate struggle.

The weapon's barrel was pointed directly at the Moon Man's heart!

CHAPTER [4]
A DESPERATE GAMBLE

Steve Thatcher stared past the deadly shotgun barrel at the stern and dogged face of the bulldog detective. Keanan was a good man, fiercely dedicated to the force. Too dedicated, at the moment, to shit Thatcher's needs. The Moon Man did not relish gambling his life against such loyalty. But he had little choice.

"I just saved your life, friend," came his muffled voice from the shell mask. "If that deserves a slug in the back, then go ahead and plug me!"

"I don't want to shoot unless I have to..." Keanan began. But the silver-headed phantom had already turned from the detective, running after the killer dogs. The business end of the shotgun followed the swiftly moving figure. Keanan's finger began to squeeze the trigger. His arm muscles tensed against the recoil which would follow the weapon's discharge.

"I don't want to shoot unless I have to..."

Then the costumed criminal vanished from sight in the shrubbery. Keanan lowered his unfired gun.

"Damn," he muttered. "McEwen'll have my hide for this."

Following the dogs' trail was child's play for the Moon Man.

Snapped branches and trampled grass led in a straight line to the tall hedge bordering the estate. From that morning's reconnaissance, Thatcher knew these shrubs hid a wire mesh fence; furthermore, he knew of a break in the fence at exactly the point where the dogs went. Earlier, Thatcher considered it a fortuitous escape route. Now he realized more than luck was responsible for the man-sized gap.

He squeezed through, coming out on the lip of a highway skirting the estate on this side. The spoor he'd been following vanished on the black-topped roadway. The dogs were nowhere to be seen. The only movement was that of a blue roadster speeding off in the distance.

Across the road another roadster was parked, the one used exclusively by the Moon Man for his sensational exploits. Ned Dargan sat anxiously behind the steering wheel. Seeing his boss, the ex-pug flung open the passenger door; when the figure with the globular head stopped to stare down the road, Dargan climbed out of the light roadster to join him.

"Hey, Boss, what's up? Where's the loot?"

"Angel, did you see four large dogs come this way?"

"Yeah. I thought there was something funny going on. This blue roadster pulled up real sudden, and I was scared whoever was in it would see you. Then these dogs come out of nowhere, jump in the rumble compartment, and they take off again like a shot."

Steve removed his Argus helmet and black cloak, handing the garments to his confederate. Frustration lined his face. "Too late to follow them now," he muttered. "They could've taken any of a dozen turnoffs by now."

"Something special about that car, Boss? I didn't get a good look at the driver or the guy with him. They were all bundled up."

"Those dogs just killed two Midwest guards and stole the show money!"

"What? Say, Boss, it's a good thing I memorized the license plate numbers!"

Steve Thatcher's face brightened. "Angel, you're an angel! What is it?"

"AN-603." Dargan's face reddened at the praise. "Heck, Boss, it's you who always tells me to keep a sharp out."

"And this time you did great!" Handing Ned his gloves, Steve urged him towards the car. "You'd better beat it out of here now. We'll meet at the usual spot near headquarters."

Angel barely had time to start the perfectly tuned motor and roar down the highway when Steve heard shouts from the other side of the hedge. The car's tires sang loudly as it screeched around a sharp turn. Steve drew his police pistol and fired into the air.

McEwen pushed his way through the brush behind Thatcher, followed by a half dozen uniformed coppers.

"Did you get him, Steve?" asked the grizzled veteran.

"I'm afraid not, Gil. They were too fast for me."

"But it was the Moon Man, right?"

Thatcher holstered the automatic and shrugged his shoulders.

"I can't say for sure. I heard the shots out front and got there in time to see four German shepherds making off with the show money, as crazy as it sounds. I chased them this far, but a car was waiting. It was a slick job, all right. But I never actually saw the Moon Man."

McEwen tipped back his hat and sighed.

"Well, I've got one man who did, and I owe Keanan a chewing-out for disregarding the shoot on sight order out on that crook. This is weird one, Steve! Two men torn to bits by mad dogs, over twenty grand stolen right from under our noses, and to top it all off I've got a wounded detective who claims the Moon Man saved his life! Can you beat that?"

"Don't be too hard on Mark, Gil. After all, he was in pain..."

"Yeah, I know," McEwen growled. Then the lieutenant's eyes narrowed. "Say, how did you know it was Mark that was hurt?"

"How? Oh, I passed him when I went after the dogs. He didn't look too badly off, so I continued my pursuit. I don't think he saw me, though." Steve spoke with outward calm; on the inside, he nervously chastised himself for the careless slip.

"If he did, he didn't mention it." McEwen shook his head to clear it. "I'm sorry, Steve. I don't mean to doubt you. This thing has me shook. Do me a favor, will you? Don't tell Sue I've been treating her fiance like a prime suspect. Okay?"

"Sure, Gil. How about we stop at Rosie's on the way back to headquarters? We both could use a cup of hot java."

"Yeah, coffee and a head shrink. I think the whole world's gone nuts!"

CHAPTER [5]
THE BLUE ROADSTER

Several minutes of traveling at an incredible speed through the sparsely settled suburbs of Great City came abruptly to an end as the blue roadster suddenly slowed. The car pulled into a driveway with a screech of tires. A sign facing the road indicated that the gritty path led onto the private property of the Morganstal Kennels.

The vehicle edged around the main building, an old-fashioned wooden frame house overdue for a fresh paint job. It finally came to a halt alongside a dark brown sedan.

Beyond the two cars lay the screened quarters where the kennel's dogs should have been lodged. Every cage was empty. It was a strange kennel that lacked any canine population at all.

But the only dogs were the four German shepherds who now sprang from the rumble compartment of the blue roadster. Close behind them walked a pair of truly weird characters.

The first was a tall, lean man with an imperial air in his carriage. Even a casual observer could tell he was accustomed to being obeyed. The shadow of a wide-brimmed hat his hid his face, and wore a heavy gray overcoat with the collar turned up. It was an unusually warm wardrobe for such a mild autumn afternoon.

The dogs leapt about him playfully as he walked. That these happy, innocent pets could have played any part in the brutal events of a quarter hour ago seemed inconceivable.

His companion had the torso of a giant. He would have towered over the first man but for the fact that his legs ended about the knees. Yet he hobbled along quite well on the stumps without apparent effort or discomfort. His scarred face expressed only a mindless contentment.

Tucked under each of his arms was a bulging gray moneybag.

Bostiff was this creature's name, and he served with unquestioning loyalty the evil genius which the world knew only as Doctor Satan.

Satan signaled the dogs to leave him. The animals cheerfully romped among themselves in the backyard. Ignoring them, the two men entered the small but neat Morganstal house. Bostiff dumped his burdens on a wooden table in the kitchen. On its surface was a blood red cap from which extended two curved horns.

"We did it, master!" he cried in triumph. "We did it!"

Satan removed his bulky outer clothing and turned his veiled face on his man-servant. He picked up the red headpiece and adjusted it over his face mask. Penetrating black eyes shone with relentless fury through the mask's eye slits.

"Not without interference, you fatuous dolt!" he spat.

"The Moon Man, master?"

"Of course, the Moon Man, Bostiff! I must have foiled his own attempt to grab the receipts. The fool! He'd have been welcome to the cash if he'd stayed out of it. Money is of no importance in itself. The whole point of today's exercise was to demonstrate my powers, a demonstration he may have undermined by killing two of my hounds. I cannot help but feel this mystery man poses a threat. I shall have to take his actions into account before they disrupt my plans more seriously."

"What shall we do?" asked Bostiff, concerned that his master should suffer even a slight annoyance.

"Nothing, provided he does not bother me again. I've more important matters to deal with. On the other hand, should he persist in being a thorn in my side, I will have to pluck him out."

"Bostiff will kill him for you, master."

"If necessary. For the time being, dispose of those foul beasts in the yard as you did all the others. Their usefulness to me is ended. Then use this excess cash to pay off Captain Dushorfer at the piers, and deliver the remaining equipment from his warehouse to the castle. I will be there after dusk, and when I arrive the second phase of my operation can commence. I have some details to finish up here first."

"The two in the cellar?" Bostiff smiled unpleasantly.

"Yes. They remain drugged until I am ready to deal with them. Have no worries on that account, Bostiff. Doctor Satan has waited too long for this moment to let anything go wrong."

The crippled giant barked a chilling laugh. He knew exactly what his master intended for the prisoners below, as soon as the sun went down.

Scooping up the sacks of money, Bostiff shouldered open the kitchen door. The happy yelping of the dogs pervaded the house, then grew soft again as the door slammed behind the cripple.

Two minutes passed, and the beasts' voices were stilled forever.

Doctor Satan listened to the screech of the roadster as it tore out of the driveway. When it was gone, he turned to stare at the shabby plywood door which led to the cellar stairs. He stood thus in utter silence for one eternal moment. His coal black eyes were bright with fiendish anticipation, and his hands itched eagerly beneath his crimson gloves.

"You thought to defy the powers of darkness," gloated the arch fiend. His harsh whisper was addressed to the unconscious forms of his basement captives beyond the thin barrier. "For that reason I wait for sunset to impose your doom. It is fitting that you die in darkness, defeated in the one element you devoted your life to fighting." Though two lay at his mercy, they were but one enemy to his mind.

Beneath the crimson mask, Doctor Satan's mouth twisted in an evil grin. Tonight would be a gone one for the Lord of Terror.

CHAPTER [6]
"SOMETHING BEYOND OUR EXPERIENCE!"

"**A**h, that is good news. Yes, thank you for calling, Doctor. I appreciate it."

Chief of Police Peter Thatcher replaced the telephone next to a cardboard cup, half-filled with cold coffee, on his ancient roll top desk. He shifted in his easy chair to face his plainclothes detectives. Gil, along with the Chief's own son, Sergeant Steve Thatcher, was waiting anxiously for the old man's report.

"That was the hospital," the Chief explained. Lines of worry etched his face, making him look much older than his fifty plus years. "Keanan's wound was deep but fleshy. No major damage, but he'll carry scar tissue the rest of his life. Given a few stitches and a couple of weeks for recuperation, he'll be back on his feet again and ready for light duty."

"That's good news, dad," Steve replied. "Mark's a good man."

"There are two more good men decorating slabs in the morgue, Sergeant! Both of them retired members of this force!" Gil's voice shook with unrelieved tension.

"Back off, Gil," Chief Thatcher ordered. "Steve meant no disrespect to those men."

"Oh, dang it! I know, Chief. It's just that this case has me buffaloed." The grizzled veteran shoved a cigar into his mouth. The stogie remained there unlit, a monument to his frustration. His teeth dug angrily into the tip.

"Do you think the Moon Man is the culprit, Gil?"

Steve's throat went dry when his father voiced that question. He bent forward, listening to McEwen's reply with renewed alertness.

"My own prejudice tells me, sure as hell, it's just the kid of caper he'd go in for. But..."

"Go on," prompted his superior.

"You know how it is after so many years on the force, Chief. You have an instinct about these things. I'd love to nail the Moon Man for this, but my gut feeling says no. The style is all wrong. He's a loner. I've never known him to work with anyone but Dargan. Certainly not with animals. And he's only killed that one time that we know of. He's not about to take unnecessary risks."

The Chief bent forward and lifted a manila enveloped from his desk. He offered it to the flint-eyed detective.

"Ballistics says the bullets from the dogs's bodies match precisely some samples we know to have come from the Moon Man's gun on other occasions," he said. "Except, of course, that time he got his hands on your automatic, Steve."

The younger Thatcher smiled weakly. He remembered that day, early in the Moon Man's career, when an expert from the department's ballistics lab revealed a bullet from the criminal's gun had markings identical to those from Steve's police weapon. He'd been lucky to discover that in time to cover his trail, and since that day the Moon Man used exclusively an anonymous weapon salvaged from a criminal hide-out during a routine raid.

"This report," his father continued, "proves conclusively that the Moon Man was on the grounds at the time of the robbery. And, of course, we have Keanan's testimony to corroborate it."

"I don't deny he was there," McEwen argued. "Bit it doesn't make sense if you think it out. If he was using the dogs, why kill them? And why just two out of the six?"

"They you believe Mark's story," Steve put in hastily.

"I have to. Oh, that crook was there for the cash, all right, but those killer pooches beat him to the punch."

The Chief scratched his chin thoughtfully. "Then we're up against something new this time," he whispered softly. "Something completely beyond all our experiences."

McEwen yanked the cigar from his mouth, nodding vigorously. "Exactly! A person or persons unknown who trains animals to commit daring crimes. I'm already working on that angle. My squad is compiling a list of every known dog and general licensed trainer in and around Great City right now. It won't take us long to make the rounds, asking questions. Every cop on this force wants to make it hot for those killers. If we're lucky, we might even wrap this up by morning!"

"I hope so, Gil," the Chief sighed. "For all our sakes. The Clarion has a special edition on the streets already, thanks to some Press Radio Bureau reporter, and I'm afraid it'll cause a panic. Commissioner Sutton himself called to emphasize his concern, so you know how serious the situation is."

Chief Thatcher's words weighed heavily on all three men. Each knew that their jobs over the next few hours would demand the utmost of their abilities, and each prayed inwardly for the strength to meet this challenge.

"Hey, I've got to finish typing my own report!" Steve said abruptly, rising from his chair. He lifted a weary hand to stifle a yawn. "I'd better get clear of the paperwork and grab a bite to eat. Se you later, dad, Gil."

Both policemen mumbled farewells, preoccupied by their own thoughts. Thatcher paused just outside the door of his father's office, closing the door behind him.

Perhaps he should not have withheld the license number that Angel had noted. Such information could save Gil and the plainclothes division hours of exhausting legwork. But there was no way now that he could bring it up and not conflict with his prior story. Besides, if there were any chance for the recovery of that money, he meant for it to reach the poor and needy of Great City, as he'd intended from the start. The Moon Man could hardly accomplish this goal if he was threatened by police interference.

Shrugging his shoulders, the debonair detective continued down the long narrow corridor of thin and drafty doors until he reached his own private, tiny cubicle.

CHAPTER [7]
SATAN'S PRISONERS

To the world at large, Ascott Keane was a wealthy young playboy who squandered his time on the polo fields of the very rich. And at one time his lifestyle justified that harshly critical description. But Keane possessed a super-intellect which would not let him be content with the frivolities of his social peers.

He applied his talents to the study of one branch of science after another, until he mastered them all. Then, still restless, he turned to the black arts and supernatural lore.

During this phase of his learning, Ascott Keane grew aware of the continual struggle between the forces of good and evil existing on all levels, from the most mundane to the errantly esoteric. In the grip of this awakening realization, he vowed to enlist all his special skills in this eternal war.

As an independently wealthy agent and criminologist extraordinaire, Keane waged his fierce personal combat against the many faces of evil. He'd barely begun his career when he met his greatest challenge, and became chief adversary of the world's most powerful criminal genius.

At this moment in time, however, Ascott Keane felt very little like a super-sleuth. He was just regaining consciousness in the face of a dull and lingering pain. His eyes burned; his head throbbed to twice its normal size; his throat was filled with cotton. Like an alcoholic hangover, he mused cynically, but without the consolation of a night before.

Finally he forced his gray eyes to open against glaring lights, which made them tear. Vague shapes gradually formed before his blurred vision as his drugged mind took in the surroundings.

He was in a long, dark room. From the cool damp of it, he judged it to be a cellar. The floor was cluttered with boxes of various sizes and several machines of unfathomable purpose.

Keane tried moving a hand to shield his eyes. Restraining metal bit into his wrist. He glanced up and behind. His hands were chained to the wall by a pair of steel bracelets above his head, two feet apart. He was a helpless prisoner.

Then he grew aware of a soft, shallow breathing in the room that was not his own. He glanced to his left. Chained in the same fashion, only inches from his side, was his girl Friday, Beatrice Dale. Her head lolled to the right, so that her chin rested against the shoulder nearest Keane, cradled by an upraised arm. Beneath the disarrayed strands of dark brown hair, the woman's face was composed in sleep.

One name thrust itself into Ascott Keane's thoughts as he strove to piece together his situation.

Doctor Satan.

Now fully alert, Keane allowed his memory to race back over the events of the past twenty-four hours.

A postal mark on an otherwise obliterated envelope found at the scene of the archfiend's Chicago defeat had led the master criminologist to Great City as the next site for Satan's horrible brand of evil. Beatrice and he had left at once, checking in to the Continental Hotel at the heart of the city. Here they begun a methodical hunt for the villain. They pored through local newspapers over breakfast for indications of anything remotely unusual. During the day they split up, checking out strange items and familiarizing themselves with the town to determine likely hideouts. Each night they met, tired and discouraged, to compare notes in Keane's room. The day concluded with dinner and a study of the afternoon and evening papers.

The fruitless search lasted almost two weeks.

Last night's heavy rain had cut short their leg work. After an early dinner in the hotel restaurant, Keane accompanied his lovely assistant to the door of her suite.

There an odd thing happened. Beatrice's key turned easily enough in its lock, but the door would not open. Keane put his shoulder to the barrier, pressing hard. In spite of his athletic strength, the door did not budge.

There were no hotel personnel in the hall, as Ascott led Beatrice to his own room. She sat comfortably on the edge of his bed while he picked up the house phone to call the manager.

A yellow-gray vapor shot from the mouthpiece of the instrument as the sleuth raised it to his face. He felt his knees buckle, his stomach churn sickeningly. The room seemed to cave in on him. The last thing he saw was Beatrice's shocked reaction as she leapt from the bed for the door to Keane's room.

So obviously she hadn't made it. The knock-out gas spread rapidly.

How long had they been here? Hours, Keane guessed from the cold numb feeling in his arms. The question was irrelevant. They were at the mercy of a fiend.

Mercy! The word was singularly inappropriate. Doctor Satan's evil frame lacked the remotest semblance of scruples.

A low moan came from Keane's left. Beatrice was coming to.

She blinked her eyes and spoke in a thick, lethargic voice.

"Ascott? Is that you? Where are we?"

Keane started to reply, but only soft and incomprehensible mutters escaped his lips. He was properly gagged with a red silk handkerchief. This time, Satan had not underestimated his foe's ability to free himself with a spoken incarnation; he'd used the simplest method at his disposal to counteract that power.

They were at the mercy of a fiend.

But Beatrice Dale's question did not go unanswered, though she would wish it had. Out of the basement's gloom stepped a crimson-clad figure, moving stealthily, making barely a sound. A chill voice issued from the figure's grotesque, immobile mask, a voice she knew all too well, in reply to her desperate pleas.

"Where you are makes little difference, Miss Dale. Very soon, nothing of this world will make much difference to your or your employer."

Doctor Satan's fiendish laugh filled the dismal room.

CHAPTER [8]
A PLEASANT SURPRISE

A visitor was waiting for Sergeant Steve Thatcher to open the door which bore his name. Without warning, a pair of arms wrapped themselves tightly around the debonair detective's neck. Warm lips pressed rapturously against his. Recovering from his surprise, Thatcher returned the kiss. Then he pulled back for a long admiring look at the pretty features of his fiancee, Sue McEwen.

"Now, that's what I call an hello!" Steve said, gently disentangling himself. "You should come by more often, honey."

"Oh, Steve, darling! I heard all about the dog show. Why, you could've have been caught!"

Aside from Ned Dargan, Sue was the only living person to know of Steve Thatcher's dual identity. She respected his noble intentions and kept his criminal career secret from even her father, though she knew how the older man fretted over the Moon Man's exploits.

"Now, Sue," Steve chided softly. "You know I have to take these risks. Too many people suffer and die each day because they lack the bare necessities of life. Where could they turn, without the Moon Man's aid? How can I weigh my private happiness against all that human misery?"

The woman snuggled against his chest. He placed a comforting arm around her shoulders. She was shivering.

"What's wrong, darling?" he asked.

"I'm scared for you, Steve. Those horrible dogs, killing those men like that! What if it had been you?"

"But it wasn't. And I'll know what to expect the next time."

"Next time? What do you mean?"

"Sue, whoever trained those dogs is sure to strike again. This is only the first round. He'll have to be put away before someone else is hurt. If the police can't get him... it'll be up to the Moon Man to make things hot."

She straightened, pulling away from Steve. But the clean-cut detective refused to let her go. He brought her close to him again.

"Honestly," she said with feigned exasperation. "I don't know who's more stubborn, you or my father."

Steve laughed. "That must be why you love us both."

"In spite of that, you mean. Now kiss me goodbye. I told dad I was coming down to the station, and if he doesn't see me soon, he'll think I've been kidnapped and send the whole radio squad out looking for me."

They shared a last embrace. A moment later, only the delicate scent of her perfume remained to counsel Steve Thatcher.

The young man stood reflecting for a long moment. Lieutenant McEwen's little girl was quite a woman. He considered himself extremely lucky to be engaged to her. Fiercely loyal, she would one day make a fine wife. One day, when the Moon Man could in good conscience retire from his perilous career.

His eyes flitted to the wall clock over his desk. He hadn't realized the hour was so late. Already, it was growing dark outside.

Duty first. He reluctantly forced all thoughts of the pretty blonde to the back of his mind, settled into a straight-backed chair, and picked up his telephone. He clicked several times to get the operator's attention.

"Switchboard," answered a nasal voice at last.

"This is Sergeant Thatcher. Connect me with Motor Vehicles, in City Hall, please."

"Thank you, sir."

The connection was made quickly. A gravel voice burst suddenly onto the line.

"Motor Vehicles," it said.

"Jim, this Steve. I need a favor."

"I owe you one, pal. Name it."

"Can you give me the owner of a blue roadster, license number AN-603?"

"It's a snap. Hold on a minute."

When Jim spoke again on the phone, Steve dutifully copied down the pertinent information. Then, thanking his friend, the detective broke the connection. With one hand he thumbed through a copy of the Great City phone directory, stopping at the middle.

Again he clicked the phone and requested the operator to dial an outside number. He kept the receiver pressed to his ear for a full minute without speaking, then hung up.

Steve's report on the dog show robbery had actually been completed before the council of war was called in his father's office. He removed that report now from the top drawer of his desk and placed it conspicuously on top of his blotter. Then the Chief's son left his office and the turreted headquarters building for the night.

Or so he thought.

Angel was parked at the prearranged rendezvous point, a narrow side street two blocks from the station house. The ex-pug watched Steve approach in the rear view mirror, but cautiously did not greet him until the idealistic detective climbed in beside him.

"Hi, Boss. What'd you find out?"

"Plenty, Angel. The car you spotted is registered to a Paul Morganstal of 212 Water Drive. That's the South End district. I checked the phone book, and it's legitimate. The same address is given for the Morganstal Kennels, a pet training school specializing in guard dogs. And the phone is out of order."

"Sounds like big trouble, Boss."

"That's how I see it. Drive along the West Highway. That'll get us to the South End in ten minutes."

The last rays of sunset faded into black as Angel flashed on the roadster's headlights, brightly illuminating the narrow street. The finely-tuned motor purred into life like a contented kitten. Seconds later, the car rolled smoothly off in the direction of the nearest highway ramp.

CHAPTER [9]
THE DEADLY RAY

Hatred flared in Ascott Keane's icy gray eyes as the red-mantled figure of his sworn nemesis stepped noiselessly from the shadows, like the grim spectre of death he so garishly represented.

"Doctor Satan!" gasped Beatrice Dale in a voice that was barely a whisper. Her throat constricted at the awful sight of that expressionless mask.

"Of course, Miss Dale," he answered with caustic courtesy.

"Who else possesses the genius to ensnare so formidable an opponent as Ascott Keane?"

A small workbench separated the fiend from his captives. On it rested a grotesque piece of machinery. Satan's gloved hands brushed lightly over the knobs and lights dotting the gadget as he paced behind it. The cruel eyes animating the mask kept the helpless pair in constant view.

It was maddening for Ascott Keane to stand so close to his hated foe, the enemy of all mankind, and still be powerless to lay a hand on him. The criminologist ached to encircle that loathsome evil neck with his bare hands and twist it into oblivion. His muscles tensed with frustration. He tugged at his bonds, but the steel bracelets only bit deeper into already raw flesh. Satan's eyes glowed triumphantly at the futile gesture.

"It has been a long campaign, Keane," the master of menace conceded. "One I think we can both be proud of. But at last the contest nears its climax, the only one possible. I am the victor. We both knew I would win, didn't we?"

Keane fixed the soulless mask with a cold stare, refusing to even acknowledge the question with a head shake. Satan tore his eyes away, disquieted by Keane's rectitude. His gloved hand reached decisively for his machine's controls.

"Look upon your death, Ascott Keane!" he gloated.

A switch snapped into place. The machine hummed wildly.

Two small glassite balls on either side of it glowed with an eerie white light. A think silver rod, inserted in the contraptions's lid, stretched out toward the prisoners.

"My latest inv..."

A sudden metallic clatter interrupted the villain's exposition. Satan glared at the basement ceiling, alert to any follow-up sound. When he was satisfied that all was once again still, he turned his attention back to the bound couple. A short, inhuman chuckle escaped his lips.

"Rescue, my dear Ascott? I think not. More likely some stray cat, free for the first time to explore these kennels unmolested. As far as you two are concerned, the point is academic. Nothing interferes with the grim reaper's engagements, and I've placed your names in his book for an appointment at dusk. The sun has only just gone down."

"You fiend!" Beatrice burst out angrily. "Someday you'll pay for your crimes!"

"Perhaps, Miss Dale. But not today, which is unfortunate for you and the man you chose to ally yourself with."

Satan's fingers pressed under stud. A ruby beam of light shot out from the tip of the silver rod, which served as the barrel of the bizarre weapon. The beam struck a point on the wall a foot to the left of the pretty secretary.

Beatrice's eyes widened in horror, and she cringed inwardly when she saw the concrete and brick foundation of the basement hiss, crackle, and melt around a tiny hole at the spot where the light touched it.

Now the crimson-clad criminal turned a knob at the back of his sinister device. The silver rod drifted so slowly that its movement was almost imperceptible. The red line of high intensity heat carved a deep, smoking furrow, inching along the wall toward the chained woman.

"It's a death ray, Keane," Satan explained casually. "Using the power of refracted light rays. I thought you'd enjoy the simplicity of it, the subtle touch of the mundane that I've added exclusively for your benefit. You can't see the results very well from where you are, can you? I assure you, it's working perfectly. But don't take my word for it. Miss Dale will be pleased, no doubt, to inform you the precise moment it starts cutting her in two!"

The woman tried twisting her body away from the encroaching line of doom, but her bonds allowed her little slack. She could gain only a couple of extra inches. At its present steady rate of progress, the beam would reach her in less than three minutes.

Three minutes to an agonizing death! A gasp of horror fell from her lips at the thought.

The sounds of her struggles drove Keane's savage fury to a new peak. All his strength surged through his body. The former playboy bent every ounce of will to the task, pulling against the steel clamps until tiny rivulets of blood ran from his wrists to stain the cuffs of his stiff white shirt.

It was hopeless - the chains were too strong!

Less than six inches now separated the auburn-haired girl Friday from a horrible end. Her courage in the face of such impossible odds gave way to a whimper of fear. Beatrice screamed, and her piercing shriek filled the dismal cellar with an additional splash of terror.

Satan clasped his hands in glee. Feverish excitement flooded his eyes, betrayed itself in every gesture. His chilling laugh was a macabre contrapuntal note to Beatrice's desperate cry.

Then a third voice came from the shadows behind the emperor of evil. Doctor Satan whirled around at the sound of it.

"Okay, Mister Red Robes. You've had your fun. Turn that thing off, now!"

CHAPTER [10]
A BATTLE OF WILLS

"This is the second time you've chosen to meddle in my affairs," Satan greeted. He bowed his head in mock deference to the automatic with which the intruder threatened him.

Ascott Keane could not say which of the pair had the more startling appearance - Doctor Satan in his melodramatic blood-red robes and horned death-mask, or the black-cloaked figure with the frosted glass dome covering his head.

"I said turn off that infernal machine!" repeated the Moon Man. The business end of his automatic pointed to the death ray.

"Whatever you wish, my celestial colleague," the master fiend conceded. His voice dripped with unction. "But first, wouldn't you like to put that silly plaything away? It could go off and hurt someone."

"That's the general idea, Mist... hey... what the...?"

The Moon Man's arm moved downwards in stiff, jerky motions. He saw rather than felt the limb lowering, watched disbelieving his body rebel against his mind. He staggered back a step, regained himself, lifted the weapon again to menace the evil genius. Once more the arm wavered and dropped.

"Your arm is heavy, Moon Man," Satan intoned. "You can barely hold the gun. You will feel much better if you lower your arm."

Ascott Keane, himself an expert hypnotist, recognized the power Satan invoked in his attempts to control the Moon Man. He knew the evil doctor's abilities first-hand. They were irresistibly potent. Yet the thief in black was somehow holding his own against that control.

"Down, I command you! Lower your gun!"

And then Keane realized the reason for the Moon Man's uncanny resistance lay in his bizarre helmet. Optimum hypnotic control depended on eye to eye contact. Concealed by the Argus glass, the Moon Man had the advantage of this barrier to Doctor Satan's will. They were stalemated, though Satan's superbly developed mental powers would soon overcome this minor obstacle unless the Moon Man received additional support.

Keane closed his eyes tightly to drive the horrifying plight of his secretary from his mind. Bound and gagged as he was, he could help their would-be rescuer only via telepathy. He bent all his concentration toward transferring waves of mental energy across the darkened void of the cellar.

Fire the gun... fire the gun... fire the gun...

Steve Thatcher felt like a psychic swimmer, trapped between two mighty currents, desperately seeking escape from the raging rivers of his mind. One current would drag him to certain doom; the other promised safety. But which was which? How could he be sure? His gun arm throbbed painfully as he fought these pressures.

The edge of the sinister ray licked at Beatrice Dale's tweed jacket. The heavy material began to smoke.

"Lower the gun, Moon Man!"

Fire! Keane's mind insisted. Fire the gun! Fire! Fire! Fire!

An ebon-gloved finger tightened on the trigger of the automatic. The echoing roar was followed immediately by a brilliant explosion. The death ray machine, its vitals torn by steel-jacketed bullet, erupted in a ball of flames.

"No!" cried Satan in dismay as his dreams of easy victory turned to ashes. But his alarm was short-lived. Flames from the wreckage licked at the dry timber of the cellar's support beams.

Exhausted by the battle of wills, the Moon Man had collapsed to the floor. Seeing this, the fiend resumed his familiar gloating tones.

"Fools! he raved. "You think you have eluded your deaths.

Look at the flames! You've only exchanged my way of dying for a slower and more painful one! Farewell, Ascott Keane!"

Doctor Satan bounded over the limp but conscious Moon Man, and up the narrow cellar stairs. His insane laughter was swallowed by the hideous crackling of the inferno.

Thick clouds of smoke billowed through the chamber. The silver-headed phantom struggled to his feet.

"Hurry," Beatrice urged, seeing the Moon Man's sluggish recovery. "Set us free, or we're all lost!"

The criminal stumbled past the gutted ruin of Satan's devilish machine. His hand pressed against the wall that had been so deeply scarred by the ruby beam. Oppressive heat seeped beneath his robes and helmet. Sweat poured down Thatcher's face.

"No time to look for a key," he gasped after studying the locks on the woman's binding bracelets. "I'll have to shoot them off. Close your eyes!"

Beatrice turned her head, clamping her eyelids shut. Two loud reports rang out. Her arms dropped lightly to her sides. She felt a stinging sensation in her wrists, and rubbed them to restore circulation.

"Now free Ascott," she bade. "Quickly!"

Again, two well-aimed shots were fired. The tall man sagged against the wall, no longer supported by the bonds. The mental conflict had weakened him as well, more so than the Moon Man, who'd merely acted as vessel for the awesome powers. Beatrice grasped Keane by the arm, helping him to remain erect. Her delicate hand pulled the silk gag from his mouth.

"My thanks to you, Moon Man," the sleuth gasped. Hungry lungs sucked in the rapidly thinning air.

Steve Thatcher looked at the holocaust surrounding them. The stairs were ablaze now, and the coal chute was far too narrow to crawl through. Satan must have previously spread some inflammable substance around, possibly gasoline, for the house to catch fire so quickly. He'd no doubt intended its destruction after murdering Keane and the woman.

Unfortunately for the three, Doctor Satan's foresight was serving him in exceptionally good stead.

"Save your thanks," Thatcher advised breathlessly. "I think we've had it."

Within minutes of the utterance of those portentous words, as explosion rocked the crumbling walls of the death chamber. Flooring from the kitchen above crashed down. With a fearsome groan, the weakened frame of the house began to give way.

It was only a matter of seconds before the entire structure was engulfed by a massive, all-consuming flame.

CHAPTER [11]
FLAMES OF TERROR

Ned Dargan crouched silently on one knee, hiding among the thick hedges siding the grounds of the Morganstal Kennels. He kept a sharp watch on the small frame house the Moon Man had entered. High above, a brilliant half moon cut lazily through the night sky, scattering wispy clouds in its path.

He tensed when the single gunshot rang out, but the Boss had ordered him to keep his place. Besides, one bullet did not indicate an exchange of gunplay, and the ex-pug had confidence in the man he worked for. The Moon Man would not fall victim to an ambush without getting off a shot himself.

Then four sharp cracks pierced the air. Angel would wait no longer. He drew a short-barreled revolver from the pocket of his overcoat and stepped out onto the moonlit driveway. The burly fighter gave no thought to his own chances against whatever mysterious foe lurked within the darkened house. If the Boss was in trouble, it was his duty to rescue him with no questions asked. Steve Thatcher alone had saved Ned Dargan from poverty and starvation, accepting him as the Moon Man's secret emissary. He would willingly sacrifice his life for the detective.

Quickly, Dargan crept across the gritty driveway to the back porch, following the same course that Steve had minutes earlier.

He paused at the first of the three narrow wooden steps leading to the screened door. A deep, explosive rumbling from inside the building startled him. When all was silent again, Dargan took another slow and careful step up.

The door before him suddenly slammed open. Dargan had to leap backward to avoid being struck. He stared in consternation at the figure which now stood in the portal, a man draped in scarlet. The face was hidden by a flat crimson mask with long, extruding horns.

Although he was thrown off-guard by the abruptness of the confrontation, Dargan had been keyed up, expecting something every moment of his approach. He recovered quickly. The pistol leapt up in his crusty hand, to aim at the heart of the outlandishly garbed stranger.

"Don't move an eyelash!" the ex-pug warned.

"This grows tiresome," Doctor Satan muttered irritably. He raised his red-gloved hands well above his head, but not as an idle gesture of surrender. His fingers snapped together sharply, and several archaic, unholy syllables escaped his lips.

An inexplicable lightness flooded Dargan's body. His mind shut down. To a casual observer he might seem to be suffering a catatonic seizure, standing only because his leg muscles were locked into place.

Satan stretched a hand forward to push the entranced ex-pug out of his way, then changed his mind. Wherever possible, he preferred dupes

"Don't move an eyelash!"

and underlings to perform necessary mundane tasks for him, leaving his creative mind free for more important contemplations. Satan was not a man to let an opportunity slip by. He could make some use, at least, of this muscle-bound oaf.

"Put that gun away," the masked man ordered. "Then go over to that sedan and get behind the wheel."

Ned unhesitatingly pocketed the gun, walked to the brown sedan parked near the empty dog cages, and slid into the driver's seat.

Doctor Satan climbed in the passenger side.

"Now, my malleable giant, start the car. We'll be taking the West Highway out to Notingham county."

Ned turned the ignition key with a crusty hand and eased the clutch back. The sedan's engine came to life smoothly, its headlights creating eerie shadows in the darkened kennels beyond.

Like a machine, Dargan backed the vehicle down and out of the driveway, onto the concrete roadway called Water Drive. The area was brightly lit by the conflagration enveloping the Morganstal house, and on other cars were visible.

The distant wail of sirens promised that the street would not remain deserted long. Some neighbor had seen the flames shooting into the night and called the fire department. The police, too, would soon arrive to investigate such a terrible blaze.

"Faster, you witless puppet!" hissed Doctor Satan. "We must be off, before the authorities get here!"

A squeal of rubber on asphalt rent the night. The brown sedan was soon swallowed up by the darkness.

By this time the house was a mass of bright red and yellow tongues of fire, reaching ever higher. Ancient timbers crackled and groaned their death agonies. The aged structure yielded to its inevitable cremation. Supporting beams gave way with a tremendous roar. The peaked roof crashed inward, caving in the floors below.

Neighborhood dogs, aroused by the fearful scent of doom, mingled their excited baying with the crackling of burning wood and the clamorous sirens of approaching fire engines and police radio cars. The howling added an uncanny, almost profane note to the ghastly scene.

They might have been the hounds of hell, claiming their due.

CHAPTER [12]
THE BLUE LIGHT

"**S**ave your thanks," was the Moon Man's advice to Ascott Keane. "I think we've had it."

There was little reason to believe otherwise. The cellar was a raging inferno, and the spreading holocaust made an ever-shrinking circle about the three. Thick, suffocating smoke rapidly gobbled at what little breathable oxygen remained.

"Help me to my feet," Keane ordered. "There is still a chance!" His voice carried a compelling note of authority.

Between them, Beatrice Dale and the Moon Man brought the lanky sleuth to an erect posture from the spot where he had slid down along the wall. Once there, Keane stood by himself, although his long, powerful fingers still gripped their arms tightly in case he should falter. The muscles of his firm, large mouth drew tight in intense concentration.

"There is one way to save ourselves, and I must employ it now, before the smoke overcomes us."

Keane's words sounded distant. He was speaking with only a small fraction of his mind. The rest was engaged in gathering his resources of psychic strength.

"You must both take hold of my shirt and keep that grip!" he commanded. "Whatever happens, do not loose your hold on me, and do not speak. I require the utmost concentration for what I am about to do. Is that clear?"

Beatrice smiled. The tall and beautifully formed secretary had complete faith in the man she worked with. The Moon Man inclined the glittering sphere of his head. Each grasped the shirt, as directed.

Keane had not waited for the acknowledgements. The occultist's light gray eyes, set deep under coal-black eyebrows, turned upward unseeing. Long, strong hands stretched above his head. He chanted in unfamiliar but deliberate syllables.

"Oh Holy Sirilon, hear my plea! Holy Sirilon, I beseech the powers of the Blue Light. Yasta moot, Sirilon, yasta reen."

A soft blue glow radiated from Keane's upraised palms. The Moon Man started at the sight, but heeded his strange ally's injunction not to break contact. The alien words, begun in a barely audible whisper, gradually grew louder - and as they did, the lambent color spread outward, claiming more territory. It engulfed Keane completely, and continued expanding until his two companions were also encased. It gave an eerie blue tincture to the Hades raging about them.

"Yasta moot, yasta reen. I beseech the powers of the Blue Light!"

Steve Thatcher was thoroughly discomforted by the experience. Enveloped though they were by an elliptical sphere of weirdly glowing light, he felt no physical sensation. At least, he felt no new sensation, for something he had felt was now missing.

He was no longer aware of the fire's burning heat! The perspiration which had beaded on his forehead now felt coolly damp, almost clammy! This alien light, magically invoked by a man he'd just rescued from certain death, somehow protected them from the harmful effects of the flames.

Completing the spell, Keane moved quickly to the cellar stairs. He kept his hands raised and continued to mutter the arcane words, but the pitch had leveled off. The Blue Light was established, it only needed to be maintained.

The stairs had not yet been consumed, though brightly ablaze. The trio clambered up them hurriedly. The charring wood could not long bear their weight.

They were nearly out of the cellar when Beatrice stifled a scream. The top step gave way beneath her left foot!

But her right heel was firmly planted on the floor above. With an assist from the Moon Man, she swiftly regained her balance. Her tapering hands retained their grip on Ascott's shirt.

An instant later, the cellar beams gave way. The floor of the kitchen collapsed in a deathly roar.

The route to the back porch was now impassable. Keane led his companions along a short, narrow corridor to the adjoining front room. Here, too, the fire was blazing merrily, licking along carpets and up draperies. The floor boards were also weakening, but for now were still sturdy enough. Keane's invocation continued as they passed through the front door of the ill-fated structure and out onto the open porch.

Clear of the lethal house itself, Keane suddenly ceased his spell and let his arms drop. The blue light vanished as swiftly as a balloon punctured by a hat pin. All three of them leapt from the porch to the relative safety of and overgrown grass plot.

Another explosion rocked the air, just before the entire house cave in on itself.

The escapees stood several yards from the scene of carnage, ankle-deep in dew-soaked lawn. Dazzling red and yellow bursts filled the skies. Billowing clouds of black, ugly smoke blotted out the stars. Sirens and bells competed with the hideous crackling as the first of the fire-fighting engines pulled up.

Neighboring houses brightened with curious lights.

Beatrice leaned her coppery brown head against Ascott's strong and comforting shoulder. Now that the immediate danger was over, she released her pent-up emotions. Full awareness of the horror they's so narrowly eluded made her feel faint. It was good to have someone strong to hold on to.

"It's over, Beatrice," Keane assured her.

"I know, Ascott. But we came so close to... to being..."

"But we're still alive, thanks to our timely friend..."

Ascott turned to the empty spot where, a moment earlier, the Moon Man had been standing. Their mysterious savior now had melted into the night. The couple had no chance to search for their benefactor, for a crew of Great City's fire-fighters was charging across the lawn. Some bore axes, others carried long and snaking hoses which gushed thick streams of water. Three wore bulky asbestos suits. A few barked orders as they passed, urging Keane and Beatrice to the safety of the street, but these men had no time to see if they were heard and obeyed.

More trucks pulled up, as well as a fire chief's car and several police radio cars. On the fringe of all this activity sat the ominous, thick armor-plated vehicle of the bomb squad.

Under this valiant onslaught, the smoldering blaze would sooner or later have to submit.

Leading Beatrice by an arm, Keane wound their way through the tangle of official vehicles while avoiding any interference with the heroic civil servants who were risking their lives. One pair of steely gray eyes took the time to follow their progress.

As the couple unknowingly neared their watcher's radio car, the owner climbed out to confront them. He was a bulldog figure of a man. His grim, leathery face expressed extreme displeasure. He made no effort to hide from Keane and Dale the fact that he'd had a rough and tiring day. And he expected it to get rougher before it was done.

"I'm Lieutenant McEwen of the police," he barked. His teeth drove hard into his unlit cigar. "Who the devil are you people, and what in blue blazes is going on here?"

CHAPTER [13]
KIDNAPPED!

Four blocks from the ruins of the Morganstal house, on a tree-lined side street well out of sight of the police and fire-fighters, the Moon Man cautiously approached his light roadster. A quick survey through the sheen of his mask assured the silver-headed phantom that the street was empty. And alert and inquisitive eyes within the nearby houses would be focused on the fire. He removed his Argus helmet, blackened by soot and smoke, to peer more closely into the car.

The driver's seat was vacant.

"Ned?" he questioned, looking towards the shrubbery lining the inside edge of the sidewalk. "Are you here?"

No answer came. Steve Thatcher pulled open the car's rumble compartment, unlatched the black leather case which he found in there, and slipped the halves of his helmet into it. His eyes searched the darkened street again, glowing with concern. It was not like the ex-pug to walk off in the middle of some action. It was not like him at all.

"Angel?" he whispered, responding to a rustling of leaves. A gray cat shot across the road from beneath a rose bush.

Steve threw the rest of his Moon Man regalia into the case and latched it shut. Where could the affable giant have disappeared to? Sure he would not still be at the site of the monstrous conflagration! Not with police and firemen combing the area!

A chill crawled along his spine, echoing a gloomy thought. Could Angel have entered the flaming building to save him, and fallen victim to the same grim death that Steve had so narrowly escaped? That was something the ex-fighter would do, in spite of Steve's standing directive for Angel to flee if a situation became hopeless.

On further reflection, the detective decided against that possibility. He'd have heard that deep, powerful voice calling him even over the roar of the pyrotechnics, for Ascott Keane's protective shield did not filter out sound. Instinctively, he felt Angel still lived. They'd been together too long, shared too many tight spots, for Steve not to know in his heart his friend was dead. He had no such feeling.

Even as he dismissed that thought, another and in some ways more frightening one crept into his consciousness. That fiend in crimson, so gleefully planning the cold-blooded murder of the couple in the cellar, almost took control of the Moon Man's mind.

Could he have succeeded with Ned Dargan? If so, some unguessably nasty fate surely awaited the faithful Angel. The Moon Man may have helped save the lives of two complete strangers, only to lose his most loyal and trusted friend.

A worried Steve Thatcher locked his roadster securely and walked back toward the carnage of the kennels. He could not drive to the panic-filled scene in a car identical to that known to belong to the Moon Man, particularly as Thatcher himself owned no such car. He would have to pick it up later, when things had quieted down.

Steve's progress was slowed by the throngs of nosy housecoated citizens thickening behind police barricades. Past the latter, he spotted a black and white radio car. The sight raised a flicker of hope in his heart. If Dargan had been captured, at least he was still alive, and Steve could plan an escape for him. At the worst, the police might have seen Ned or the mysterious figure in red. He pushed his way through the crowd in a bee-line until he reached the barricades. A flash of his gold detective's badge allowed him further passage to the site of the disaster.

Three people, known to Steve, stood out in the confusion, their faces tinted bright pink by the light of the flames: the tall, athletic frame of Ascott Keane, the equally tall and lithe Beatrice Dale, and Thatcher's tenacious superior, Gil McEwen.

"Gil!" Steve cried out in surprise. "What are you doing here?"

The plainclothes honcho returned the astonished look. "I should ask you the same question, Steve."

"I was on my way to meet Sue for dinner when I heard the sirens. I thought I could help, so I ordered my cab to follow."

The explanation sounded plausible, and Steve did in fact have a standing dinner engagement with his fiancee - an open invitation for occasions such as this. If questioned, the pretty blonde would back up his story.

"I'm afraid you'll have to skip that date, Steve," Gil replied. "Sue'll understand, having a cop for a father. I'll need all the help I can get to sort this out. This guy is Mister Ascott Keane, and the lady is Miss Dale, his secretary. Folks, meet Sergeant Steve Thatcher. One of my best men."

Steve accepted the compliment with an embarrassed laugh, shaking the strong, powerful hand which Keane offered him.

"I'm sure that you're quite an unusual young man, Sergeant," the occultist said.

"These people have had a bad time of it," McEwen continued. "Their story is they were kidnapped by a gangster called Doctor Satan, and barely got clear of both him and this fire with their lives."

"Thanks to the Moon Man," Keane added, smiling.

Steve started to open his mouth, but McEwen cut him short. "Don't ask!" he begged. "It sounds whammy enough!"

"All right," Steve agreed. "But why is Great City's ace detective answering a routine fire call?"

"I'm not, really. We were headed this way before the alarm sounded, Steve. The body of a man was found in a downtown alley at about noon. The death was handled routinely, as most of the squad was working on the dog show heist. That is, it was routine until the morgue report, with his identification, crossed your father's desk. That was just after you left us."

"And who was he?" Steve asked.

"Paul Morganstal. The man who owned this kennel."

"How horrible!" Beatrice exclaimed, tightening her grip on Ascott's arm.

"You can say that again, Miss. Especially the way he was done in. That was the clincher, Steve. The body was literally torn apart. From loose hairs and denture marks, the lab figures he was killed by at least four large dogs. Possibly more."

Cold hatred flared in Ascott Keane's normally placid gray eyes during McEwen's speech. When he opened that firm, large mouth to speak, the amateur sleuth's words dripped with a venomous loathing.

"Doctor Satan has claimed yet another victim."

CHAPTER [14]
HUNTINGTON'S FOLLY

Perched on the lip of a dreary cliff top which overlooked the murky and treacherous Murder River was the ancient English castle commonly referred to as Huntington's Folly. At first hearing, this would seem a specious name for the grim gray fortress jutting up into the clouds, majestically imposing itself against the skies, a sentinel of stone and mortar watching over the dim and distant lights of the metropolis; but given the strange history of the structure, a more appropriate moniker would be difficult to imagine.

Immigrant Wilbur Huntington had arranged, through luck and shrewdness, to be in the right place at the right time to capitalize on the sudden growth of the railroads. By 1901 he was a millionaire several times over, with more money and leisure time than a poorly educated pub-keeper's son knew what to do with. One day towards the end of that year, the octogenarian sat looking out of the panoramic windows of his elaborate townhouse, pondering the architecture of Great City (then dimly lit by gas lamps) and the overpowering cliff side in the distance. And suddenly he realized that all he wished to do at this stage of his life was recapture the carefree days of his youth, when he scrambled happily through the green fields of Cheshire county in England. His adopted country had made him wealthy, but it could never really feel like home without an authentic English castle.

With that decision, he employed trusted agents to travel all over Great Britain in search of a suitable castle which he could purchase, disassemble, and ship stone by stone to be rebuilt near his second home in Great City. At the same time he bought a hundred acres of the barely arable land which included the cliff top, and renamed it Notingham Estate.

Wilbur Huntington was not the first wealthy man to conceive of such a grandiose plan, nor would he be the last. Scores of castles, both imported and copied from original plans, dotted the landscapes of the eastern states - particularly throughout New England - by 1937. And the fate that befell Huntington's dream was, sadly, not uncommon.

The citizenry of Great City thought the idea mad right off.

Imagine moving a British castle so close to a modern metropolitan area! What purpose could such a childish impulse serve?

Only Wilbur Huntington could have answered that question, but he was unable to. He did not live long enough to enjoy his dream. One week before the millionaire's 97th birthday, the date on which the castle would be officially be ready for habitation, the old man suffered a coronary attack. He lapsed into a coma from which he never recovered. The doctors speculated that the excitement and anticipation caused by the castle might have been directly responsible for his death, and the newspapers quickly picked up on the notion. So it was that the project was dubbed Huntington's Folly.

After the magnate's passing, a handful of surviving relatives attempted to take over the estate. To their surprise and bitter disappointment, Huntington's lawyers revealed that all of the millionaire's vast holdings had been liquidated to finance the purchase, transportation, and reconstruction costs. What funds remained for maintenance of the building and grounds were woefully inadequate. Six agonizing months of struggling to keep the project viable were more than enough for the relations. Both lands and castle were donated to the state for use as a museum.

The tourist department valiantly promoted the ancient fortress complete with stone turrets and suits of armor. They fared no better than the private owners. The estate was located deep in an isolated woody area, far from major highways, and the rough access roads were impassable in poor weather. The effort was abandoned with the advent of the Great War, and the furnishing distributed to state museums or sold to private collectors. The castle was boarded up. A single caretaker stopped by, once a month, to discourage vandalism.

It remained closed for over two decades.

A fortnight prior to the dog show incident, a man named Wilson turned up at the state property office to inquire about the structure's availability. Wilson was a small-time real estate agent, representing a fabulously rich client whom he was naturally eager to please. This client, he explained to bureaucrat after bureaucrat, had seen the castle from a distance and wanted it as a sort of hermitage. The buyer valued his privacy highly, and would pay handsomely for the privilege. After much discussion, Wilson handed the county clerk a certified check for double the true worth of the property. The deal was completed. That same day Wilson telephoned his client at a prearranged time and confirmed the sale. His job was over.

It should be pointed out that Wilson was a thoroughly legitimate realtor. The generosity of his client's retainer made it easy for the agent to dismiss irregular behavior as merely eccentric, and exaggerated proof of the purchaser's desire for seclusion. Throughout the entire transaction, Wilson had no personal contact with the man he represented. All details were conveyed via the mails or a voice over the telephone which may or man not have belonged to the castle's new owner. He received final payment in the form of a series of postal money orders, endorsed with the fictitious name of Elias P. Hudge.

Not for a moment did the realtor suspect he'd actually bought Huntington's Folly for the world's greatest criminal mastermind, and his lack of curiosity turned out to be quite a healthy trait. Had he perceived the slightest inkling of what really happened, Doctor Satan would not have suffered him to live.

CHAPTER [15]
THE MOON MAN REVEALED!

The crimson-shrouded figure of Doctor Satan paced the main hall of Huntington's castle in a bitter rage.

"How could they have escaped that fire trap?" he ranted, throwing up his arms. Coal-black eyes glowered from the slits of that impassive mask. "How? How?"

Bostiff had no answers for the tall, gaunt man. The crippled servant even regretted having told his master what he'd overheard on the police band radio frequency during his trip from the Great City docks. The dispatcher clearly stated the Morganstal Kennel disaster had claimed no lives; all three occupants at the time managed to flee before the building collapsed. Satan did not have to guess the trio's identities.

"How?" the criminal repeated. His gloved fist crashed down on a workbench near the massive fireplace which warmed the dank and disused interior. Bostiff dragged in the last of the gear from the pier shipment and then stood off to the side, swaying hideously on monstrous arms as thick as most men's thighs, watching his master apprehensively. He disliked acting as a bearer of ill tidings. The rightful ruler of the world should not have to contend with such petty details.

Glimpsing Bostiff's cowering frame, Doctor Satan seamed to suddenly become aware of the spectacle he was creating.

"It does not matter," he concluded with an abrupt calm. "I won't make the same mistake twice. When the Moon Man crosses my path again, he shall die."

"Yes, Master," agreed Bostiff, pleased that Doctor Satan was once more in control. His thick lips grimaced grotesquely.

"I have work to do," Satan added. "Is this all the equipment?"

"It is, Master."

"Good. Begin assembling it as I've instructed. The radio transmitter - is it operable?"

"Yes, Master. The antenna is already set in place along the turret on the roof. You can broadcast whenever you wish."

"Excellent. I'll do so after I've had a few more words with our unexpected guest. I've a feeling I can make good use of him before disposal becomes necessary."

The freakish Bostiff nodded and set to work, tearing open a large wooden crate with his powerful hands and sorting the electronic components within. Satan watched the legless brute, his black eyes glittering demonically, until the work seemed well under way. Only two men ever served Doctor Satan, if they could be called that; the mighty Bostiff and a hairy, monkey-like oaf named Girse. Not wanting to bring both underlings to Great City, Satan had left Girse behind this time, as Bostiff's mechanical acumen would serve him better on this project. He was satisfied he had made the right choice. Then the diabolical figure in red strode to a small, dark antechamber adjoining the main hall. Originally, this room served as storage space; now it contained only a thick-chested ex-boxer named Ned Dargan. The man squatted cross-legged in a far corner. His eyes were glazed over, still under the trance which Satan had put him in.

"Good evening, my rather stupid friend," Satan greeted. He inspected his prisoner carefully. The trance still held firm. Dargan was an excellent subject. No reinforcement would be needed.

The fiend's voice grew cold and commanding.

"I could read your simple mind easily, but it amuses me to hear you speak at my will. You will answer my questions."

"Yes," croaked Dargan. There was no hesitation in his reply save that his throat was parched. The ex-pug could no more resist the masked fiend's probe, even on the deepest levels of his mind, than an ice-cube could keep from melting under an August sun.

"Who are you?"

"Angel."

"Angel?"

"That's what folks call me."

"Ah, I see. A nickname." Satan's voice was almost gentle, hinting at a tender deadliness.

"Yeah."

"Tell me your real name."

"Ned Dargan."

"Now, tell me, Ned Dargan, what you were doing near the Monganstal

"Then tell me, Ned Dargan, as you value your life and sanity!"

Kennels earlier this evening?"

"Waiting for the Boss."

"And who is the Boss?"

"The Moon Man."

Doctor Satan caught his breath at this stroke of fortune. His suspicions that the man might prove more useful alive than dead were confirmed. This prisoner was indeed a prize catch.

Satan could perhaps conclude the affair of his larcenous rival sooner than he'd planned. Already, several diabolical plans wormed their way into his twisted mind.

"If you work for the Moon Man," the sinister voice droned, "then you must know who is behind that shining mask."

"Yes. I know."

"Then tell me, Ned Dargan, as you value your life and sanity! Tell me who the Moon Man is!"

"He is Detective Sergeant Steve Thatcher, of the Great City Police Department."

Satan clasped his gloved hands together, rubbing them gleefully.

"Very good, my fortuitous slave. Rest now. I will have work for you soon."

Dargan lapsed again into a senseless coma as the figure in the guise of death glided from the tiny room, trailing his cold, malicious laugh.

CHAPTER [16]
SATAN'S ULTIMATUM

"Doctor Satan is beyond madness in his aims and goals - an icily, brilliantly sane and ruthless monster, who will stop at nothing to achieve his evil ends. His presence here in Great City can only spell disaster.

Steve Thatcher sat transfixed on a folding chair up in his father's office, listening. Ascott Keane concluded his fantastic report. Also present and equally fascinated by the account were Chief Peter Thatcher and Lieutenant Gil McEwen. Keane's secretary had been taken to the McEwen home to stay with Sue after her harrowing ordeal.

All three felt the importance of Keane's warning. Chief Thatcher had already contacted several police departments in New York, Detroit, Chicago and other cities where the criminologist had foiled even more incredible plots. He received nothing but praise of the man's abilities. If such a formidable sleuth feared Doctor Satan, the criminal was truly a foe to be reckoned with.

McEwen shoved a cigar into his mouth and scratched his chin.

"Let me get this straight, Keane," said the leather-faced veteran. "You say this Satan character doesn't commit these crimes for the loot?"

Keane sipped coffee from a cardboard cup and nodded. "Not exactly, Lieutenant. There is always a profit motive behind his offenses. But he doesn't need the money. Doctor Satan, whoever he is, was fantastically wealthy to start with. He has unlimited resources for organizing his schemes. These sensational crimes are a whim of ego, a thrill-seeking test of his skills against the law."

"The same way you use your skills to aid us," Steve suggested.

Set deep under coal-black eyebrows, Ascott's gray eyes sparkled. "An interesting comparison, Sergeant. One I've often made myself. We may be two different sides of the same coin. Certainly, we're well-matched."

"What do you suggest we do, Mr. Keane?" asked Steve's father. His voice sounded very old.

"For the time being, nothing."

"Nothing!" McEwen exploded. His cigar spun crazily between tightened lips.

"We have nothing to go on," Keane explained. "So we wait. From Satan's past performances, I can safely say the events so far are only a prelude to his real plans."

"A prelude!" the Lieutenant repeated. "Robbery, kidnapping, assault, murder - what's left for him to do?"

As if in answer to Gil's question, there was a sharp rap on the office door. The white-haired Chief called out a reply. A thin, wiry desk sergeant poked his head in on the council of war.

"Begging your pardon, sir," he apologized. "We're picking up a strange call signal on the radio. It's jamming out all the regular wavelengths. I think you better hear it yourself."

"Very well, Anderson, thank you. Carry on with your duties. Gil, turn on that set behind you."

McEwen complied, twisting the knob. A shriek of static filled the room, and then a cold and sinister voice drowned it out.

"...peat, this is Doctor Satan, the new master of Great City. I take this opportunity of addressing my subjects to announce my first demand."

All heads turned to Keane. Hard marks ridged the criminologist's cheeks, and his firm mouth became a black slit in his face.

"It's Satan, all right," the sleuth confirmed. "I'd know that voice anywhere."

Words of menace continued crackling over the air waves.

"The tragic event at the Community dog show this afternoon was only a small sample of my power, citizens of Great City. I can command at will every dog within city limits. I can control their simple minds, enslave them to my slightest whim. Every loving, devoted pet in your city will become a savage, brutal killer when I so choose.

"Think heavily on this, people of Great City. A child's warm and furry friend! A blind man's seeing eye dog! Even police trackers are not immune! The kindliest master will not be safe from his beast's raging blood lust!"

"He's crazy!" McEwen blurted out. "Nobody can do that!"

"Quiet!" Keane hissed. "There's more."

"Listen carefully, good people. A tribute of six million dollars will be delivered to me no later than noon tomorrow. I will contact your Chief of Police shortly before the deadline with delivery details. If my demand is met, catastrophe will be averted.

"But should anyone, including your noble police force, interfere with this transaction - you all shall know the fury of Doctor Satan!

"It is now almost midnight. Should there remain any doubt of my ability to fulfill this threat, let the following prove otherwise."

The radio went silent. In the Chief's office, the grim-faced crime-fighters waited tensely. So, too, did millions of other Great City inhabitants who had also heard the broadcast of terror.

Outside the Chief's open window, a dog started barking. A second joined the howling, and then another and another until it sounded like every canine in the city was baying at the top of its lungs.

The terrifying cacophony lasted five full minutes. Just as it seemed that human ears could take no more, the beasts ceased yelping as suddenly as they'd begun.

Chief Thatcher fell back into his easy chair. His wrinkled face turned white with despair.

"Lord preserve us," he whispered softly. "That madman was telling the truth!"

McEwen's fingers drummed nervously on the arm of his chair.

His teeth drove hard into his stogie. "There must be something we can do?" he growled.

"Usually," Keane said, "I advise against making these blackmail payments. But this scheme is more complex and far-reaching than his others. I suggest we begin collecting the ransom money. Satan will have to contact you personally, and that may give us a lead."

"You're the expert, Keane," said the Chief. "But I hate to give in to that monster without a fight!"

"We aren't giving up, Chief Thatcher, but the safety of millions of innocent people must take priority. I cannot protect them all from Satan's insidious machinations."

McEwen grunted. "If we only knew where he was hiding out!"

"Perhaps I can be of some help, Lieutenant," came a muffled voice from the open doorway.

McEwen, Chief Thatcher, and the supernatural sleuth known as Ascott Keane turned as one to face the ebony-cloaked, silver-headed form of the Moon Man!

CHAPTER [17]
AN UNLIKELY ALLIANCE

The notorious criminal stood just inside the door of Chief Thatcher's private office. The weird Argus helmet reflected the tiny white moon of the single desk lamp - another justification of his bizarre soubriquet.

McEwen, the relentless, hard-faced, stony-eyed hunter of wanted men, rose from his chair. His hand leapt for his holstered automatic.

"Don't try it, Lieutenant!"

The Moon Man extended a gloved hand from the ebon folds of his flapping cloak. The blue muzzle of his own gun glinted in the his grip. All three men in the room were covered.

"Sit down and listen!" ordered the silver-headed phantom. "What I have to say won't take long!"

Steve Thatcher was putting all his chips on this gamble. The easy part was slipping out of the office to his own cubicle, where he'd donned the spare Moon Man regalia kept in his private locker. Now he was grateful for the events that had once smashed his helmet, convincing him to keep two Moon Man costumes handy.

Nor was it much of a trick to be back and waiting unseen, for the others were enthralled by the extortionist broadcast. The corridors were usually empty at this time of night. The fearful canine chorus had covered the sounds of his return.

So far his play was paying off. None of the lawmen had as yet noticed Steve Thatcher's absence. The Moon Man hoped to complete his mission and be gone before they did.

"I propose a truce, Lieutenant."

"Huh?" replied Gil, startled. "Did you say... a truce?"

"Temporarily, of course. Until a common enemy is dealt with. I refer to Doctor Satan."

"You want our help because Satan's putting you in the shade? You're nuts!"

"Hear him out, Gil," Chief Thatcher interjected. "What he's driving at may not be so far-fetched."

"Thank you, Chief," said the man in the globular mask. "It's foolish to scatter your resources hunting both Doctor Satan and myself. Clearly Satan is the more deadly threat, and must be stopped at all costs. Even if it meant our joining forces."

"I don't like it," McEwen growled. "How's this truce suppose to work?"

"Call off all your men currently working on my crimes. Direct all your energies to the capture of Doctor Satan. In exchange, I will refrain from any new criminal activity, and will use the underworld grapevine to come up with possible leads on my own. Anything I learn will be relayed to you or Keane.

"Agreed?"

"What!!" McEwen burst out. "Great City's Finest, working hand in glove with a known thief and murderer? Why, the day we need your help..."

"Is today, Gil," interrupted Chief Thatcher. "Take it easy. I know you're active head of this department, and my position is largely honorary, but I still rank over you. We'll do as you ask, Moon Man."

McEwen chomped angrily on his cigar. "All right, Chief! I won't go after you, Moon Man, if you stay out of my way. But only until this Satan character is in the cooler. I'll be right back on your tail a minute later!"

"Understood, Lieutenant. Good hunting."

The Moon Man punctuated his statement with a blast from his gun. The bullet smashed the bulb in Chief Thatcher's lamp, plunging the room into darkness. A silhouette figure slipped out into the hallway, dragging a hat-tree down with a black-gloved hand to cover his escape.

"Don't just stand around like wooden Indians!" Gil cried. "Get him!"

The Moon Man found and flicked off the switch for the hall lights before McEwen and Keane could stumble out of the Chief's office. The halves of the Argus helmet were quickly unhinged, bundled up in the whipped-off cloak and gloves, and stuffed into a dark corner of the janitor's closet. The regalia could be recovered after the commotion settled down.

Once again the sharp-eyed, clean-cut young detective, Steve Thatcher drew his service gat and switched the hall lights back on. His first sight was of half a dozen uniformed men charging up a narrow stairwell. Leading the onslaught was the gaunt Sergeant Anderson.

"We heard a shot!" the desk sergeant exclaimed.

"The Moon Man was here!" Gil bellowed as he reached Steve's side. "Search the entire building!"

"You can try the back stairs," Steve ordered, following Gil's directive. "I'll check out this corridor." That would give him the chance he needed to replace his gear in the false bottom of the locker under his desk.

Breathless, Steve felt a thrill of excitement build inside his chest. He had pulled it off!

"I'm on it, Gil," he said, starting down the narrow hall. "But I think we've lost him."

"Yeah, right out of our mitts. It's not the first time, either. What a guy!"

Keane chuckled at the remark. "And quite an ally, Lieutenant."

"A crook to catch a crook, Keane?"

"An intriguing proposal, at least."

"Maybe, but I don't like it one bit. Cops shouldn't make deals with crooks like that. No siree."

Steve Thatcher reholstered his gun and went through the motions of a thorough search. He wondered at his own daring. It might seem like a cheap ploy, yet in good conscience he could have done nothing else. The poor and starving people of Great City would suffer most under Doctor Satan's regime, and they were the very souls the Moon Man was inspired to aid. He had to volunteer his services and be free of police interference while he followed his own line of investigation.

Did he act wisely? Or would the truce be his undoing? If he grew careless and Steve Thatcher was revealed as the Moon Man, it would almost certainly kill his father, shatter Sue's heart, and even break as hard a man as Gil McEwen. If the grizzled detective ever learned that the notorious criminal he sought with all his heart was engaged to his only daughter, it would destroy his confidence and his career.

Steve Thatcher worried about these questions and feared the answers.

CHAPTER [18]
SINISTER SOLUTIONS

The legless Bostiff leapt clumsily into the air in his glee. His master sat calmly before the Sonar-Ray machine, a fiendish product of his own warped imagination. The blackmail broadcast had come off exactly as planned. The instrument beneath his gloved hand performed perfectly.

"Bravo!" Bostiff clapped his meaty hands together as his giant torso struck the castle's stone floor. "You showed them, Master. They'll all be running scared now!"

Doctor Satan lovingly caressed the central panel of the complex apparatus. Batteries of lights glowed soft yellow as they cooled, their energy draining for storage in silver conduit boxes. His coal-black eyes darted to his right, where the radio set with which the satanic mastermind had declared his orders was placed.

Even with the Moon Man's untimely interference, Satan's time-table for the exploitation of Great City was going as arranged. But the man in the blood-red robes was not content.

His ambitions were still threatened, and the thought nagged at him so much he even confessed his doubts to an underling; an action he normally never considered taking.

"Perhaps, Bostiff, you celebrate too early."

"But, Master, how can you fail? Those fools have no way of stopping you! They know nothing of the Sonar-Ray!"

Satan's hand slapped flat on the console with a resounding clap.

"Among those fools is my deadliest adversary, Ascott Keane. Time after time he has thwarted my plans. While he lives, I can never know complete success. I think I should deal with him immediately."

"You have a plan?"

"He must be approached indirectly, my stunted disciple. Indirectly. I'll not catch him off-guard so easily again. You will return to Great City.

Recruit a pair of local gunmen, discover the whereabouts of Keane's personal secretary, and bring her here as quickly as possible."

"Snatch Beatrice Dale?"

"Precisely. As long as she is my unwilling guest, Keane will be at my command. Yes, she will prove quite useful in first controlling the movements of my sworn nemesis, and then luring him to his final destruction. Be most careful not to harm her, Bostiff. Dead, she is of little value. Understand?"

The cripple nodded his misshapen head.

"Good. Before you go, come with me. You will enjoy seeing how I dispose of a second thorn in my side. Doctor Satan will sleep well tonight."

The archfiend rose from the console which he'd used to control dog minds. He strode across the main hall of the castle, his red robes flapping, to the antechamber containing the mesmerized Ned Dargan. Bostiff hitched after him, trailing the hem of the master's crimson garment.

Dargan still sat cross-legged in a far corner of the room. He followed his captor's entrance with glazed eyes, but their images did not register on his befuddled mind. Not until Doctor Satan willed them to.

Flaming pools of raw energy flashed beneath the eye-slits of Satan's devil mask. The Luciferous figure spoke in a flat voice, dulled of emotion.

"Observe, Bostiff, how simply I handle this business of the Moon Man. Angel Dargan, you can hear me?"

The burly ex-pug's fist-marked lip, scarred by his days in the ring, parted slowly. They were stiff and dry.

"I hear you," he answered.

"Very good. In a few minutes, Bostiff, here, will drive you back to Great City. Give him the address of Steve Thatcher's apartment and he will take you there directly. Once you leave the car, you will not remember how you got there. You will not question it. The important thing is that you go immediately to Steve's rooms and wait there. Is that clear, Angel?"

"I will go to Steve's place."

"Right. When you see Steve, you will realized that something is wrong with him. He is acting oddly. This is because he is not the real Steve Thatcher!"

"Not Steve?"

"No. He is a gangster posing as Steve Thatcher. He is an evil man. He intends to kill both you and Steve. The real Steve Thatcher may even at the moment be dying."

"Steve... dying?"

"Yes. Only you can save him. You must stop this ruthless fraud who wishes to harm your Boss. Tell me, Angel, how you will stop him."

"How... stop him?"

"Yes," prompted Satan. "You will have to kill him, won't you?"

Anger flushed Angel's scarred mug. "I will have to kill him! I will! I will kill the imposter!"

Doctor Satan wrapped an arm around the big man's shoulder in a brotherly gesture.

"Exactly, you poor dupe. The only way you can save Steve Thatcher is to kill the imposter. You are a true friend, Angel."

Bostiff turned from the ludicrous tableau to stifle his absurd giggling. What an ironic death his master conceived for the Moon Man! Murdered at the hands of his most trusted aide!

"It shall never be said," the masked man told his crippled slave, "that Doctor Satan lacks a flair for the dramatic." Satan pointed a rubber-gloved finger to the door.

The warped creature left the anteroom before his master, rolling with laughter on a stone floor thick with the dust of twenty years. This plan was too damned funny for words!

CHAPTER [19]
FRIEND AGAINST FRIEND

Dawn was just beginning to drive away the shadows of a long and terrible night when Steve Thatcher finally climbed the single flight of steps to his rooms. He'd spent a grueling three hours reviewing possible strategies with his father, McEwen, and a vaguely truculent Ascott Keane. The combined strain of the late hour and the horrible threat which hung over the city told all too well on Chief Thatcher, so Steve thought it best to see the old man home first. Then the sharp-eyed detective took a cab out to the suburban area where the Morganstal Kennels had stood, recovered the Moon Man's roadster, and returned in it to the drab tenement district housing Dargan's latest hideaway. He'd spent more time at that hideaway, a sparsely furnished room on the first floor, looking for his devoted friend. Unsuccessful, he'd finally decided to come home. The light roadster was parked in an alley nearby, where it was unlikely to attract attention.

A tired and worried Steve Thatcher looked forward to a shower and an hour's nap before returning to his duties. With Great City facing the direct peril of its existence, he could spare no more time than that.

He shifted the black leather case he carried from his right hand to his left and dug into his pocket for the apartment keys. Normally, he'd have left the Moon Man regalia in the roadster's rumble section. But with Angel missing, he felt more comfortable with the costume close at hand. Things were getting hot, and the Moon Man might be needed in a hurry.

The gentle click of the key turning in the lock did not cover the shuffling sound beyond. Someone was waiting inside.

Staying outside, Thatcher pushed the door open slowly. He stood in the doorway, silently, silhouetted against the glare of the hall light behind. He let his eyes grow accustomed to the dim interior of the room.

As far as he could tell, nothing had been disturbed. He caught his breath, seeing the great hulking from half hidden in the thick curtains by the window. He recognized the intruder at once.

"Angel!" Steve cried in relief. "Where the devil have you been? When you disappeared from the kennels, I thought..."

"Fake."

The giant moved forward slowly, evincing the same deadly calm which had won so many bouts for him in the ring, years earlier. Steve knew this attitude and gave ground before the ex-pug, confused by the hostile moves.

"Angel, what's the matter?" I'm your friend, Steve. Steve Thatcher. Surely you know me?"

"Liar." Dargan's tone was flat and deadly. "You're an imposter. You want to kill Steve and me. But I'll kill you first."

"Who told you this, Angel? Wait! Let me open this leather case. I can prove who I am!"

Thatcher was playing a desperate angle. The case contained only his Moon Man regalia, and the look in Angel's eyes told the detective that no proof in the world could convince him. But if he could slip the Argus helmet of the Moon Man over his head, the sudden transformation might jolt the ex-pug out of whatever spell he was under. Dargan was obviously being controlled by some malignant influence, which might only apply to Steve's civilian identity.

The ex-pug gave him no chance to make that move. Steve fumbled with the latch, but Ned shot forward with the speed of a cannonball. Under the force of his attack, the detective lost his grip on the case. It flew across the room, crashing against the wall. Only the thick protective padding which lined the interior kept the helmet inside from smashing to pieces.

Ned locked a burly arm around his friend's neck, squeezing the windpipe. Thatcher's police-training reflexes took over. Instead of fighting the grip, he suddenly went limp. The maneuver gave him enough extra slack for a countermove.

Dargan had to shift his weight to compensate for Steve's sagging form. The moment he was off-balance, the detective's hands shot up in a judo hold. Kicking hard against Angel's kneecap with one foot, Steve grasped the choking arm. Using the ex-pug's own weight for leverage, he flipped him into the air. The big man landed like a ton of bricks.

But Angel was not easily stopped. Especially not when he truly believed Steve's life depended on the outcome of this battle. The irony was that Thatcher's life did depend on it, though not the outcome Dargan was counting on. The ex-pug sprang to his feet lie a cat, and charged again.

Steve hoped he could avoid injuring Angel, but even his judo expertise was no match for the fighter's determined strength and stamina. Steve raced to his desk, where he kept a small handgun in the locked center drawer. He prayed, silently, that the threat of using it would be enough to halt the giant's rampage.

That plan was also doomed. Dargan was back on his feet before Steve could fit the key into the lock. There was no time for the gun.

Steve grabbed the first heavy object near him, which was the lead-based desk lamp. The fighter closed in. Steve side-stepped a powerful blow and brought the bottom of the lamp down hard against the side of Angel's head.

The big man slumped, unconscious, to the floor. Steve bent over him, examining the wound. It was bleeding, but not seriously. Satisfied, the detective took a length of rope from the regalia case - part of the Moon Man's equipment - and securely trussed up his friend.

"I hate to do this to you, old buddy," he apologized. "But it's the only way to keep us both alive."

Grunting, Steve lifted the heavy body into a chair. Then he slumped into the soft leather seat behind his desk to think things out.

Thatcher's mind raced now, for he knew he would have to act quickly. The sound of fighting would have aroused the other tenants of the building. Somehow he had to carry Ned Dargan down to the roadster without anyone seeing them. The delivery stairs should be safe that early in the

"You're an imposter. You want to kill Steve and me. But I'll kill you first."

morning, and he could stick to the shadowed alleyways outside. He would also need a more isolated place to keep the ex-pug than Dargan's tenement hideout. And he obviously couldn't go back to headquarters now; he'd have to phone in a story about picking up a lead and following it. That was basically the truth, anyway.

Once all those arrangements were out of the way, he would have to make one more phone call.

CHAPTER [20]
STARTLING DISCOVERY

Sue McEwen, only daughter of Lieutenant Detective Gil McEwen, had inherited her father's shrewd mind as well as her late mother's strikingly good looks. Clearing away the last of the dishes from an impromptu breakfast in the living room, she heard the hall phone ring. She quickly excused herself from her company to answer the instrument's persistent shrill clatter.

"Hello?" she addressed the mouthpiece.

"Sue? Don't say my name out loud. No time to explain. Is Ascott Keane there?"

"Ste...? Yes. Yes, he is. Beatrice is helping him dope out a strategy for handling Doctor Satan, and I'm giving what help I can. Dad just left for headquarters to fill in the nine o'clock shift. He told me about that crazy stunt the Moon Man pulled. Really! Going off half-cocked like that! He could've been captured!"

"But I wasn't. I love you, Sue. But right now I must talk to Keane. Please put him on."

Receiver in hand, Sue walked the few steps to the open double-doors which led to the living room of the McEwen residence. Keane sat on the broad couch, hunched over a map of Great City which overhung the coffee table before him. Beatrice saw Sue's signal and interrupted the master sleuth's cogitations. Keane knew the woman would not disturb him except for important matters, and moved briskly to the phone.

"This is Ascott Keane. Who am I talking to?"

Steve draped a handkerchief over his end of the phone to mask his voice.

"This is the Moon Man, Keane. I have information regarding Doctor Satan. But I need your help. Can you meet me?"

"Name the place."

"There's a string of warehouses along South Street, off the river. One of them was recently repainted bright red. I'll be inside. And, Keane..."

"Go on."

"I'd rather keep this between ourselves."

"I understand. I'll come alone."

There was an abrupt click at the end of the line, indicating the Moon Man had finished talking. Keane pronged the receiver of the hall phone and returned to the living room. Beatrice was pointing eagerly to various places on the Great City map, asking Sue to identify them.

"I have to leave for a while," Keane told them. "I may have a lead on Satan."

"Be careful, Ascott," Beatrice cautioned.

"I will. Continue what you're doing. Sue knows Great City better than we do. Together you may turn up something on your own."

With those words, Keane shrugged on his jacket and left the private home.

From their vantage point behind a clump of bushes, Bostiff and his two henchmen watched Ascott's sudden departure with a keen interest. The cripple stifled a triumphant laugh. A clear field lay before them.

The local gunmen exchanged significant glances. This mysterious, physically warped creature was a man neither would have cared to meet under other circumstances. But he paid twice what they usually hired out for, in advance, so they asked no questions.

Reaching forward with thick, ape-like arms, Bostiff pulled himself toward the house. The gunsels followed. They'd thought a cripple would be a tremendous handicap on this snatch job. But a lifetime of practice allowed Bostiff to command greater speed using only his arms than most men could summon with two sound legs. His hirelings had to run to keep pace.

At Ascott's instructions, all doors and windows were locked. Such measures were of course useless against a direct assault by Satan. But the master of evil often used underlings while he directed full attention to a project like the ransom of an entire city. With a little urging from Beatrice Dale, the pert young blonde followed his orders.

One window, though, escaped her notice. It was the window of the ground floor bathroom, seemingly too small to admit a full-grown man.

Even for Bostiff's stunted form, it was tight squeeze. But once he gained entry to the McEwen house, he slipped silently into the adjoining bedroom. There he unlatched a second window for his gunmen. Together the trio stalked the peaceful home.

"I don't see how Ascott expects me to come up with anything my father hasn't," Sue was saying. "The police are searching every possibility with a fine-tooth comb."

"Maybe some fresh coffee will help," offered Beatrice. She took the pot from the sidebar and headed for the kitchen, passing the couch where Sue was pondering. A black spot of ink, hidden until the blonde had shifted the map, caught her eye.

"What's that black rectangle down in the corner? she asked.

Sue bent closer to it. "That? I don't know. It's outside the city limits, so I've been ignoring it. Let's see... this is the cliff fronting Murder River... of course! It must be the old castle!"

"A castle?"

Sue gave Beatrice a brief history of the structure, then exclaimed, "That would be just the place for someone as melodramatic as you say Doctor Satan is!"

"And the cliff side elevation gives him the widest possible range for whatever device he uses to control the dogs," added Beatrice.

"Very clever, ladies."

The two women whirled to face the open doors. There the legless cripple stood between his two bull-necked hirelings, a hideous tableau framed by the door jamb.

"Ascott Keane would be proud of you," Bostiff continued. "Don't' try any foolish moves with the coffee pot, Miss Dale. Doctor Satan wants you alive, but I have no such instructions regarding your companion."

One of Bostiff's aides brandished an evil-looking blackjack.

Both waved their ugly guns menacingly.

"Don't worry about us," Sue whispered. "My life is unimportant if you can thwart Satan's plans."

"No," replied the auburn-haired beauty. Her adventures with Ascott Keane had taught her to stay calm in the face of danger. "It would serve no purpose. I'll go with you quietly. Leave Miss McEwen alone."

She addressed the cripple, coolly ignoring the pair of killers. Bostiff shook his misshapen head, smiling crookedly.

"She knows about the castle. She has to come with us. My master will decide how to deal with you both."

Beatrice turned to Sue. Both women were pale, the color drained from their faces. But neither would admit their terror to this grotesque parody of a man and a pair of cheap hoods.

"After you, Sue," Beatrice said, shrugging with a practiced casualty.

CHAPTER [21]
A CITY'S RANSOM

Gil McEwen fidgeted in the over-stuffed visitor's chair set next to Chief Thatcher's ancient roll top desk, his eyes shifting from the venerable old man to a bulging carpetbag set on the top of that desk. His fingers drummed a muted staccato on the cushioned arm of the chair. An unlit cigar clung tenaciously to his lips, dangling by the fragments of the its well-chewed tip.

"Blast it all, Chief!" he complained. "I've got me combing every damn corner of the city. A dozen patrolmen are sweeping through the sewers, even, at this very moment, and the waterfront districts have been covered three times over! I've pulled in every third-rate cop pounding a gas-house beat to help with the search! The whole city is bottled up! There's just no place where Satan could set up the equipment for a job this big, except by pure magic!"

"According to Ascott Keane, that's not entirely out of the question," the white-haired Chief grumbled back. "But I agree with you, Gil. Something of this magnitude requires a lot of room. Where is Keane, anyway?"

"I left him and that doll of his, Beatrice Dale, at my house. He said he needed a quiet place to think, and you know as well as I that headquarters is anything but quiet today. I don't know what he's got to think about, though. Actions' what we need. On to of the massive search and rising panic, every two-bit hood in town is using Satan's threat to launch his own private crime-wave."

"Except the Moon Man," Thatcher reminded him.

"Yeah. I still don't get that crook. He makes a grandstand play right here in your office, and we haven't heard boo from him since. If he's going to help, I wish he'd hurry up. The entire force at my disposal, and I still haven't got enough men!"

"I know, Gil. You're doing the best you can. I only pray it's good enough against this fiend."

The sudden jingling of the telephone on the Chief's desk ended the conversation. Tense anticipation flooded the room as the old man stretched out a blue-veined hand. Before lifting the receiver, he touched a cam on a small wire dictograph which had been hooked up to the phone early that morning. Then he pressed the instrument to his ear.

"Chief Thatcher here," he answered brusquely. His eyes flicked to the wall clock above his desk. The time was 11:45.

Though he'd heard the voice on the other end only once before, Thatcher recognized its chilling edge immediately. Gil silently mouthed one word: "Satan." The old man nodded grimly.

"You have the money," the voice hissed. It was a statement, not a question. Doctor Satan did not request information he already had, and he knew Great City had no choice but to yield to his demands.

Thatcher glared at the bulging carpetbag with narrowed eyes. It had taken every bit of Commissioner Sutton's considerable influence to raise six million dollars in the short time allotted.

Even in large bills, it made an impressive pile.

"I have it, you devil."

"See that it gets to Riverview Park. There is a gazebo fifty yards from the boathouse. Your man will be inside it in exactly fifteen minutes. Need I emphasize that he should be alone?"

"Is that all?"

"A warning, Chief Thatcher. I see and hear more than you can possibly realize. If I even suspect a trap, I will loose my power. You will be responsible for the deaths of hundreds of people at the fangs and claws of their own pets!"

There was a hollow click as Doctor Satan hung up. He did not need to wait for a reply. There could be only one answer.

"I don't care how brilliant Ascott Keane claims he is," the Chief asserted. "The man's insane."

Gil leaned over the desk to read the pencilled notes Chief Thatcher had made during the conversation. "Are those the drop-off instructions?" he asked.

"Yes." Thatcher ripped the sheet from his note pad. "The call was too brief to trace, as I feared it would be. There's nothing else for it. Here, Gil. See if you can get a volunteer from the squad room to make the drop."

"To hell with that," Gil spat. "I'm making this delivery n person. I want to see what this creep looks like."

"Hold on a minute, Gil. You're too valuable to risk on this kind of a thing. If anything goes wrong, we'll need your expertise right here at headquarters."

Gil scowled. "If anything goes wrong, Chief, there's nothing I or anyone else can do to save this town. I can't just sit around here, waiting until the city is all gone for nothing. If it makes you feel any better, you can put your son in charge when he gets back. Steve's a little green, but he's got a good head on his shoulders. He'll do as good a job as I would, maybe better."

Gil stuffed the sheet of instructions into his breast pocket, hefted the weighty carpetbag, slammed on his had and charged decisively out of Chief Thatcher's office. The corners of the old man's mouth turned down.

Gil was right, of course; it was this sharp-eyed quality of the ace sleuth that earned his position as active head of the department when the Chief's advanced age made his own title mostly honorary. What could anyone do against the kind of horror Doctor Satan was capable of unleashing?

He wondered what kind of lead Steve was following, to keep him away so long.

CHAPTER [22]
CLANDESTINE MEETING

"**H**ey, you! Where do you think you're going?"

Ascott Keane turned his head to peer with calm gray eyes at a pot-bellied septuagenarian watchman dressed in a blue and gray guard's uniform. The inquirer held an ancient-looking revolver on the amateur sleuth.

"It's all right, guard," Keane answered, holding out his palms to allay suspicion. "I have a special dispensation from Chief Thatcher of the police department."

Keane reached slowly into his left breast pocket. He withdrew a folded card of pale yellow. The guard reached warily for the document. His eyes left the intruder for only a second at a time, reading the card in furtive glances. As he scanned the form, his gun gradually lowered. Finally the gun was holstered at his side. The guard returned Keane's credentials with an embarrassed grin.

"Sorry, Mr. Keane," he apologized. "Can't be too careful."

"I understand. I'd like to look around this warehouse."

"What for? The cops've been here twice since I started my shift."

"I'm following up their investigation. Have you seen any suspicious characters in the last half hour?"

"No, sir. And there ain't nobody going to slip past me."

Keane smiled to himself. His psychic probe told him a different story. "I commend your efficiency," he said, passing on to the brightly painted building.

The warehouse's interior was dark. Only the dimmest of light filtered through the narrow, dust-thickened windows below the roof cornices. Rows of shelves were packed with grimy cardboard boxes. One was lined by huge wooden crates. From behind these, a muffled voice called out.

"Ascott Keane," came the soft challenge.

"I'm here alone, Moon Man, and I dislike playing games. Show yourself."

A bizarre figure stepped out from behind the nearest crate. Only the strong reflective orb of the Argus helmet could be seen at first, creating the eerie impression of a miniature full moon bobbing about inside the warehouse. But Keane's eyes adjusted rapidly to the poor lighting. He soon saw the outline of black-robed shoulders beneath the glistening sphere. An ebon finger beckoned to him.

"I apologize for the dramatics, Keane. Despite my offer of truce to McEwen, I am still a hunted man. I must take extra precautions."

"What information do you have?"

"First I must show you something."

Keane followed the strangely garbed figure back behind the crate. The Moon Man pulled a small electric torch from the folds of his cloak and switched it on. The glaring beam spotlighted the squatting form of Angel Dargan, braced against the wooden interior of the container. A nasty bruise swelled the side of the ex-pug's skull. He was bound, hand and foot, but stout rope.

Dargan snarled as the brilliant light burned his eyes.

"Where am I" he demanded. "Where's the Boss? What have you done with him, you lousy killer? How did you get hold of his rig?"

"Believe me or not," the Moon Man explained, "this man is my loyalest, and most devoted friend. He's been eating raw meat since dawn. He is convinced that I'm a fraud who's bumped off the real Moon Man, and nothing I've done can make him believe otherwise."

Keane nodded. He bent to examine Angel's eyes. The ex-pug turned his head away angrily.

"Takes two of you to kill me, huh?" he spat. "Your type always makes double sure. Cowards! Go ahead, I ain't afraid to croak! I couldn't save the Boss. I don't want to live."

"Relax, my friend," Keane said. Then, looking up at the shimmering sphere of the Moon Man's head, he said, "I can see why you need my help. This bears he earmarks of Doctor Satan's work."

"Can you help him?" Muffled as it was, the stern and authoritative voice of Steve Thatcher could not hide his latent concern.

"I don't know. I can dispense a simple spell of mesmerism.

But if Satan used any drugs to help induce this state, I may be doing more harm than good."

"You've got to try."

Keane nodded. He leaned closer to the restrained man. Angel made a desperate attempt to pull away.

"No, friend," Keane said softly. "No one will hurt you. You're just tired. Don't you feel tired?"

Keane's voice droned on. Under the influence of his soothing words, the ex-pug's tension dissipated. His eyes still glared balefully at the Moon Man and his accomplice, but he no longer shrank from them. It was effort enough to keep his eyelids open. Keane rested his fingers gently on Angel's forehead, intoning monotonously.

The result was quite fantastic. Although the ex-pug had been physically awake the whole time, his eyes suddenly cleared as if he were coming out of a long sleep.

"Boss!" he cried out, seeing the globe form behind Keane.

"I'm swell again!" Then: "Oh, God, Boss! I almost killed you!"

"He remembers!" the Moon Man exclaimed.

"Yes," Keane confirmed, smiling in triumph. "Doctor Satan has made his mistake! He intended Angel to kill himself after you were taken care of, but his plan has failed. Now your friend can lead us directly to Satan's lair!"

The Moon Man hurriedly loosed Dargan's ropes. Introductions were hasty; all three agreed there was little time to waste.

"It will be best," Keane suggested, "if we leave separately, as we arrived. There's a watchman outside who expects me to come out alone."

"Agreed," said the Moon Man. "We'll rendezvous at the end of the street, where it crosses Davis Avenue. The light roadster parked at the corner is mine."

Then the trio parted, but only momentarily. They would face Doctor Satan together.

CHAPTER [23]
THE GLOBULE OF GANARR

Beatrice Dale head come face to face with the hideous masked visage of Doctor Satan many times in the course of her association with Ascott Keane; and twice, now, within the past twenty-four hours. The inhuman disguise was as cold and cruel as the heart of the man himself must be. She'd often felt that when

Ascott finally succeeded in unmasking the fiend, there would be little difference between the false face and the real.

For Sue McEwen, this was the first glimpse of the crimson-robed monster who now held all of Great City in an unholy grip of terror. Brave and resourceful as the ace detective's daughter was, she could not repress a shudder at the sound of the sinisterly hollow voice with which he addressed the two women.

"I did not expect a second guest, Miss McEwen. But it makes no difference to me. I'm sure Miss Dale will appreciate your company in her final hours."

Beatrice tossed her auburn locks, tilting her head defiantly. "What evil do you intend for us, you fiend!" she asked with disdain.

An evil laugh slipped from between the devil mask's motionless lips. By way of reply, Doctor Satan pulled on a silk cord which hung beside him. A curtain at one end of the room parted to reveal a pane of glass. Beyond that extended another room of the castle. The huge dividing window was one of Satan's few modifications on taking possession of Huntington's Folly.

A single man occupied the second room. Sue recognized him as the blackjack-wielder who'd assisted Bostiff in their abduction. Incredibly, the man was floating three feet off the ground. He moved around timidly, in a tight circle, pounding with his hands and feet against the sides of some invisible womb. Looking more closely, the women saw the confining barrier was not entirely invisible. The hired gunsel was imprisoned by a huge bubble shade a very pallid blue.

"The one-way mirror tends to filter out some of the color," Satan explained. "But I see by your expressions that you can still make out the shape of the mystic Globule of Ganarr."

"Can he... get out?" Sue asked.

"Not by himself. It's almost impregnable from within. If this man had some moderately powerful explosive, he might crack the globule open. Of course, the explosion's force would kill him. Still, as you're about to see, the bubble is quite vulnerable to attack from without."

A door opened into the room. Through it stepped the second gunmen. Confusion crossed his face when he caught sight of his partner dangling in mid-air. He hadn't seen his fellow crook since they delivered the women into Doctor Satan's custody.

"Watch closely, ladies," Satan advised. "This will be interesting."

The second man moved cautiously toward his partner, unheedful as the door through which he'd entered closed by itself. His hands went out to gingerly feel the bubble's outer rim. The texture gave slightly under his touch.

Seeing this, the trapped man pounded with greater desperation against the rock-hard interior. By urgent gestures, he instructed the second man to do the same. His partner in crime, comprehending, made a fist of his right hand and struck the bubble smartly.

The globule's substance dissolved into a deep blue mist on impact. The prisoner dropped a short distance to the floor, landing on his feet.

But he did not celebrate his freedom long. Both he and his rescuer suddenly clutched their stomachs in paroxysms of pain. They stumbled, doubled over. Tongues protruded grotesquely from distended cheeks. Finally their eyes rolled up into their heads to stay there, and they collapsed in lifeless heaps of flesh.

Terror etched their features.

Satan gloated over the women's horrified expressions.

"Yes," he said maliciously. "That is the one drawback. Shattered from the outside, the globule dissolves into an instantly fatal poisonous gas. There is neither antidote nor preventative for the that deadly vapor.

"Now you can better understand your own situation!"

Sue and Beatrice gasped as one. They realized with a shock that while Doctor Satan was conducting his loathsome demonstration, a similar bubble had formed about their own persons. They now floated three feet above the castle floor.

Kicking hard with the heel of her pump, Beatrice found her efforts to escape as futile as the murdered gunman's.

"I should prefer dealing with Ascott Keane personally," Satan went on, "when he comes to rescue you. As we both know he will, once I send him word of your abduction, Miss Dale. However, I may be occupied with other matters at that time. If he slips past my exterior defenses, then the Globule of Ganarr will end his meddling very neatly."

"What if he doesn't fall for your trap?" Beatrice asked.

"Suppose he doesn't believe you? Are we doomed to stay in this thing until we starve to death?"

Doctor Satan laughed icily.

"Sound," he explained, "like physical force, can only penetrate the globe in one direction. You can hear me, but I cannot hear you, and Ascott Keane certainly won't be able to. Nonetheless, I can read your lips, Miss Dale. I give you my word. You will not starve.

"Because between the pair of you, there's barely two hours worth of breathable air in your exotic prison!"

CHAPTER [24]
PAY-OFF!

Gil McEwen, that stern-faced born hunter of wanted men, turned his head slowly from side to side. His steel-gray eyes took in the total view available from the center of the gazebo, including a glimpse of Murder River. This far north, of course, it was not called by that distasteful name; only further down did its bleak rapids, growing thick and murky

"Now you can better understand your own situation!"

past the warehouse district, serve as a dumping ground for gangsters who had to dispose of a body, and earn the unpleasant name and reputation.

McEwen's mouth worked in spasms, worriedly chewing the end of an unlit cigar. In the calm of the park, it was difficult to remember the hasty precautions now going on in the heart of Great City. Dog-catchers worked double-shifts to round up every stray in the city limits, a hopeless task. Warnings to chain or cage household pets securely were broadcast by every radio station. Fire inspectors were compelled to go from door to door to repeat such warnings and see that they were obeyed, for no patrolmen could be spared from the most intensive manhunt in the city's history. But the inspectors could not cover every house, and there would always be people who laughed at and defied the grim threats. A few would remain blissfully unaware of the emergency until it was too late.

In the midst of these serene trees and grasses, the lieutenant could almost believe that all those other events were part of some horribly realistic nightmare. At any minute he would wake up in his own bed, bathed in a cold sweat, and find to his relief that there was no such being as Doctor Satan, no killer dogs, no unwilling truce with his implacable enemy, the Moon Man...

But this was no dream.

The gazebo was set in the center of a flat, open area of lawn. It was impossible for anyone to approach the detective unobserved, and equally impossible for police reinforcements to hide nearby had Gil chosen to ignore Satan's warning. The closest cop stood at the gate of the riverside park, turning back curiosity seekers who might arouse Satan's suspicions or get hurt if there were any trouble.

With such a wide-open vista spread before him, it was little wonder that the flint-eyed detective was startled by a croaking voice at his back asking, "Have you got the money?"

McEwen spun around. From the direction of the voice, he expected to see his questioner standing at ground level next to the raised gazebo. A midget would not have been unthinkable.

But the sight of the legless Bostiff supporting his ape-like torso by calloused knuckles inches from the wooden planking was one for which the ace copper was totally unprepared.

"I asked you if you had the money."

McEwen nodded, showing the grotesque creature the bulging carpetbag gripped tight in his right hand.

"Give it to me," Bostiff ordered.

"Not so fast, short stuff." The lieutenant regained his composure. "How do I know you're Doctor Satan's man?"

"Because I say I am," Bostiff retorted. "Because the master would instantly kill anyone foolish enough to try such an impersonation. Do not trifle with Satan's servants, or you will incur his wrath!"

"Too much is at stake," McEwen argued. "This is might big coin. If you aren't from Doc Satan, and he doesn't get this money, it's curtains for all of Great City. I have to give this to him personally."

McEwen was playing the first hand of a dangerous game. One wrong move could spell doom for millions of innocent people. But this plan seemed to him the only chance of capturing this nefarious blackmailer.

Bostiff swung back and forth impatiently on thick, muscular arms. His face screwed up hideously while he considered the situation.

"Very well," he decided. "The master may be amused to meet as big a fool as yourself. Follow me."

A thickly calloused hand pulled on an all but invisible latch at the base of the gazebo, opening a trap door. So this was the explanation of the cripple's abrupt appearance! McEwen followed the ape-like Bostiff as the latter swung easily down a wooden ladder, stopping at the bottom to wait for the cash-burderened detective. The tunnel leading from that spot was dark and dank.

McEwen had grown up on the streets of Great City without ever hearing so much as a hint of this underground passage's existence. Yet the tunnel they now traversed had obviously been dug scores of years ago. The grizzled veteran wondered if any of the city's secrets had escaped Satan's attention.

It was not until the bizarre pair finally emerged from a crumbling, ancient structure outside the park that McEwen could even guess at the tunnel's origins.

This building, once a simple rooming house, was now a landmark, almost a monument. Its cellar, where the tunnel ended, had been sealed off nearly fifty years earlier. This was one of the few buildings still standing in Great City that was constructed prior to the War Between the States. The secret passage they'd traversed had last been used almost eighty years ago by slaves fleeing cruel plantation taskmasters.

The irony was not lost on the hard-faced McEwen. He'd walked that historic escape route on his way to meet a man who, if his plans were fully realized, would become the most powerful enslaver of men the world had ever known!

CHAPTER [25]
DEADLY IVY

"Stop the car, Angel," the Moon Man ordered. "We can walk to the castle from here."

The glittering sphere of his head turned towards Ascott Keane, who was seated uncomfortably in the roadster's rumble compartment. The criminologist nodded grimly. Parked in a thickly shrouded section of the woods surrounding Huntington's Folly, the car should attract no attention from Satan's henchmen. And they were still within thirty yards of the imposing edifice.

Shifting the empty regalia case from his lap, Keane climbed out of the car behind his two allies.

"Do we split, Boss?" asked the ex-pug. But Keane answered before the Moon Man could reply.

"It would serve no purpose. If Satan is not yet aware of our presence, he will realize that the sight of one of us means the others are in the vicinity."

"But he thinks the Moon Man is dead," argued the costumed member of the trio. "And Angel, too. You're the only one he'll be expecting."

Keane shook his head. "It's dangerous to assume anything where Doctor Satan is concerned. In any case, his belief in your deaths can be of little help. We're better off staying together, pooling our strength against anything he throws at us. But remember to leave him to me. He's too skilled for normal men."

The three moved toward the castle. A soft incantation from Keane's lips paved their way so that they passed through the shrubbery with barely a sound. Nor were they scratched, though Dargan and his Boss observed branches of needle-sharp thorns come within a fraction of an inch from them. Keane was invoking this spell for a higher purpose than mere comfort. All three men would have to be at peak alertness, entering Satan's hellish headquarters. The slightest distraction, even from a minor cut, could prove fatal.

The castle entrance stood five yards beyond the bush cover.

They would have to run for it. There was no reason to believe their approach had gone unobserved; neither was there any reason not to. It would do no harm to remain unseen, if they could.

Keane started to break free when he felt a tug at his sleeve. The sleuth stepped back. The Moon Man lifted an ebon finger to his helmet, gesturing for silence, then pointed to the rough path which led to the castle gate.

Two figures approached.

The Moon Man recognized Gil McEwen at once, and guessed that the his overstuffed carpetbag contained the six million dollar ransom. But he'd never seen anything like the strange figure leading the detective. It was a man, or had been, though Steve Thatcher was loath to call it such. Legless, the creature propelled itself with calloused knuckles that served in the stead of feet.

"God!" Thatcher exclaimed. "What is that thing?"

"His name is Bostiff," Keane replied. "One of Satan's most loyal and devoted servants. I know even less of his origins than I do of Satan's, though I've discerned no conscious attempt to hide them. There is another; a monkey-like fellow named Girse, equally as devoted to Satan. Some unholy bond lies between them and their master. Satan has shown himself willing to sacrifice such close associated a number of times, to preserve himself. Yet they stay by him."

Bostiff and McEwen entered the castle. "Give them time to get well within," Keane advised. Each man silently counted the passing seconds, until Keane whispered harshly, "Now!"

Individually, the three tore form the cover of the surrounding shrubbery. They pressed tightly against the castle wall, inching slowly towards the gate.

"Watch sharp, Angel," cautioned the Moon Man.

"Good advice," Keane added. "There's no telling who... or what... Satan has guarding the way to his secret lair."

"You bet, Boss... arggh!"

Angel's reply was lost in a gruesome choking cry. Both men turned to their stricken companion.

"The ivy!" Keane gasped. "The ivy on the castle wall!

It's alive!"

With black-gloved hands, the Moon Man grappled the vines as they wrapped themselves around the ex-pug's bull neck, pulling at them forcefully. More vines reached out, but slid harmlessly off the Argus helmet which protected the Moon Man's own throat.

The plant held firm at first, but Steve's was a desperate strength. Finally the greenery in his hand snapped; Angel was free.

Dargan threw himself away from the wall. Sucking air deep into his lungs, he peeled the clinging strands from his shoulders and head. Dying, they offered no further resistance.

"God, Boss!" he gasped. "That was a close shave. I owe you my life again!"

"Forget it, Angel. You've saved mine, and more, often enough."

"Boss! Look at Mr. Keane!"

Ascott Keane had played no part in Dargan's rescue; neither had he fled from the clutching plant-life. While Steve and Ned were battling for Angel's life, Keane's body was being buried out of sight by the encircling vines, in a human-sized cocoon. He'd folded his hands over his throat, protecting that vulnerable area, but seemed otherwise unaware of the living trap around him.

His lips moved, speaking strange words.

"Ishtar molem avid ka! Ka! Derni sed'ma hashem mas!"

The vines' attack slowly abated. In moments, the tendrils ceased moving altogether. Still Ascott Keane was a captive under the thick layer of ivy. The Moon Man drew a knife from the folds of his cloak. The entwining leaves had prevented him from reaching for the weapon in Ned's case. But before Steve could step forward to slash the first strand of green, an amazing thing happened.

The leaves around Keane turned brown, shriveling and curling and one by one dropped off. Strand after strand loosened its grip on the occultist and fell to the ground, dead. In less time than it would have taken Steve to cut through the barrier, Ascott Keane was freed.

Keane smiled grimly. Sweat poured from his forehead, showing the strain his invocation had cost him.

"I regret seeming to ignore you, Dargan," he apologized. "I had to begin that spell at once. Otherwise, we'd have all been killed by this murderous flora."

"We understand," Thatcher replied. "Are you all right?"

"A little shaky," Keane confessed. "But not too weak to continue. I'll recover as we go along."

Together the three men entered the foreboding hideout of Doctor Satan. The full extent of the horror they would face was freshly impressed on them, yet they did not hesitate. Satan had to be defeated, even at the cost of all their lives.

CHAPTER [26]
ANGEL MAKES AMEND

Dargan and the Moon Man kept a close watch to either side, while Keane probed ahead psychically for other potential hazards. However, nothing lurked in the darkened corridors. The deadly ivy seemed to be Satan's only line of defense. They had nothing to fear until they faced Hell's messenger himself.

Still, the three knew better than to relax their vigilance. Even Keane did not wholly depend on his own paranormal senses. Satan knew how to shield himself.

A door at the end of a long corridor stood slightly ajar. Eerie blue light filtered through the thin crack. The three men stopped short before the faintly outlined portal.

"Well, Keane?" the Moon Man whispered anxiously. "Is it a trap?"

"Undoubtedly," Keane replied. "Satan doesn't make clumsy errors like this. He means for us - or any intruders - to step into that room."

"What do we do now?" asked Angel.

"We enter the trap. It's our only way of reaching Satan. We know it's a trap, which should give us an edge in dealing with whatever lies beyond this door."

With Keane in the lead, the three men cautiously entered the room. Inside, the Moon Man gasped in astonishment at what he saw.

"Sue!"

"And Beatrice!" Keane cried. His long jaw squared.

The two women were sitting as comfortably as they could manage at the bottom of their bubble-prison, eyes closed, resigned to their fate. When the voices of the men they loved penetrated the mystic substance, they sounded too good to be true. Sue McEwen's lips parted in surprise; her companion merely nodded. Beatrice had expected Keane's arrival with mixed emotions. In view of Satan's diabolical device, she'd hoped he'd arrive too late.

The shock which momentarily paralyzed their rescuers gave the tall, red-haired girl hope. If only she could signal her true plight before a rash action doomed them all!

Ned Dargan was about to dash those hopes. The ex-pug was out of his depth, dealing with the phantasms of both Ascott Keane and his Luciferean adversary. He was used to action, which the situation definitely called for.

"Don't worry, Boss," he said with assurance, approaching the bubble with knotted fists. "I'll bust them out of there!"

"Don't touch that globe!" Keane shouted.

Too late! Angel was already swinging, and in all his ring experience he had never learned to pull a punch.

Luckily, Steve Thatcher's reflexes were faster. The detective did not understand the need for further delay, but he knew by now that Keane did not utter idle warnings. The Moon Man leapt forward. His Argus helmet slammed Angel in the breadbasket, and the ex-pug fell back with a grunt. His crusty fist struck empty air, inches from the globe's outer shell.

While Angel caught his breath, the Moon Man turned his glittering sphere in Keane's direction. "What's the problem?" he asked. "What is that thing?"

"The Globule of Ganarr. It's mentioned in several arcane texts, but its secret was believe buried with the destruction of Atlantis. We could easily smash it open, but it would then transform into an instantly fatal miasma. Had you accomplished your purpose, Angel, we would now all be dead."

"God!" the ex-pug swore, struggling to his feet. "I've been nothing but trouble on this whole caper, Boss. That's twice I almost got you killed!"

"Forget it, Angel," consoled the Moon Man. "You couldn't know."

"No," Keane agreed. "You couldn't. And we'll need your help to rescue the ladies."

"Me? How?"

"The Globule can be safely broken from the inside through super-human force. I can draw sufficient strength from all of us, but only a hardened athlete's frame such as yours could withstand having all that might channeled through your system. The strain is incredible."

"I'll do anything. But how do I get inside?"

"Crouch beneath the Globule and relax your muscles. I'll do the rest."

Angel got into position. Keane made a mystic sign with his hands, intoning words in the same strange accents he'd used in the incident of the ivy. The blue bubble gently descended. For one terrifying moment, Angel thought it would crush him. Instead it enveloped him like a giant soap bubble. The process was agonizingly slow; the affable giant had to be introduced with great care, lest he tear the fabric of the Globule and destroy them all. The women clung to the sides of their tiny prison to make room for the fighter.

Then, in the blink of an eye, three captives crowded the supernatural cage.

"Sit down, Moon Man," Keane instructed, crossing his own legs in an ancient yoga position. "Dargan will need all of our strength."

Keane stared boldly into the fighter's eyes, stretching out his own long, powerful arms. Like a modern day Samson, Angel followed the criminologist's example. His scarred palms pressed flat against the Globule's sides. Steve Thatcher felt a curious and uncomfortable weakness overcome his body. There was a twinge of panic. He wanted to fight the drain on his energy, but dared not resist it. Sue's only hope lay in his complete submission to these forces beyond his understanding.

Cracks slithered along the capsule's interior, radiating from the flats of Angel's hands. The fissures ran the length of the mystic prison, growing more numerous, until at last the Globule could no longer stand the pressure. It broke open like an eggshell.

The shattered fragments melted into a harmless purple mist.

Dargan rubbed his aching arms muscles. The freed women hurried to the two men seated at the wall of the death chamber.

"Steve!" gasped Sue, putting her arms around the Moon Man's neck. She suddenly realized what she was doing, and backed away.

To think that, even in the heat of the moment, she should so carelessly reveal her fiance's most guarded secret! A worried glance at Ascott Keane and his secretary-companion reassured her somewhat. The indiscretion had apparently gone unnoticed.

Keane spoke lethargically, after a moment's rest.

"Moon Man, this last outpour of psychic energy has drained me. I will recover shortly, drawing on reserves beyond your comprehension. But you must go on without me right now. Doctor Satan will at any second do away with Lieutenant McEwen, and past experience tells me the ransom payment is no guarantee that Great City will be spared the horror he planned."

Sue's eyes widened with fear. "Father? Here?"

"We saw him being led in by a legless creature," came the muffled voice from within the glittering helmet. "But there's no time for further explanations."

"The Moon Man is right," Keane added. "Go on. I sense no further traps. I'll join you shortly."

"It's all right," Beatrice confirmed. "I've seen Ascott like this before. He'll be fine. Hurry!"

Wordlessly, the Moon Man left the chamber, followed by his devoted friend and the woman he hoped to one day marry.

CHAPTER [27]
THE SONAR RAY

Bostiff reach an apish paw into the pocket of Gil McEwen's overcoat. The ace detective stood stiffly, enduring the indignity. His steely eyes burned angrily in protest of his induced impotence. The cripple withdrew a cold, metal object.

"As you said, Master," Bostiff chortled, showing his prize to Doctor Satan. "He had a gun."

The man in the crimson robes nodded. "And now you have it, my loyal servant. Foolish Lieutenant! Do you think that Doctor Satan is such a dupe? You meddle with powers beyond your understandings! I may one day die, but not by means of such a puny weapon. You may kill him, Bostiff."

"Thank you, Master." The grotesque creature lifted the barrel of the service gat to McEwen's forehead.

"So this is how Doctor Satan keeps his word! You promised safe passage to whoever delivered the money to you!"

McEwen was startled by the sound of his own voice; the paralysis which had struck him on entering Satan's private sanctum obviously did not extend to his vocal chords.

"I promised no such thing," Satan denied. "You are here of your own volition. You forgot how easily I can read your mind. Do I have to open that carpetbag to know what it really contains? Very well. Bostiff, empty the contents on the floor."

The cripple hitched himself over to the bag which rested at McEwen's feet. He unlatched it and, with one massive hand, overturned the satchel.

"You may kill him, Bostiff."

Bound stacks of newspaper, roughly cut in the shape and size of currency, spilled out.

Satan's icy laughter echoed through the hall.

"I thought your city leaders too intelligent to indulge in childish pranks," he sneered. "It seems I over-estimated them."

"No!" McEwen fairly shouted. "This was my idea alone! I'd be double-damned if I'd let Great City knuckle under to your extortion. All right, by damn! I made a mistake. I can't deal with you as I'd wished. The money is safely hidden. I can lead you to it!"

Satan shook his head. "My orders are obeyed the first time or not at all. The switch beneath my hand activates my Sonar Ray, by which I bring doom to your entire city. Watch what your stupidity has caused!"

"Fiend! I bet you'd have thrown that switch even if you did get your six million!"

Again Satan's chilling laugh rang out. "For once you are right, Lieutenant McEwen."

The reg-gloved hand reached for the ominous control which meant panic and death for hundreds of people in the city below the cliffs.

A shot echoed suddenly through the vast castle room. Doctor Satan snatched his injured hand back in pain. He turned, glaring with coal-black eyes at his attacker. A second shot was fired, this time at the hear of the sinister Sonar Ray. The mechanism exploded in a shower of sparks.

"You!" the satanic figure exclaimed. "Them my hapless dupe failed in his mission!"

McEwen, still paralyzed, could not see his mysterious benefactor. But he could guess at his rescuer's identity. The unique sound of that voice muffled by the Argus helmet, a voice which had haunted him for months, confirmed his guess.

"You'll soon wish he'd succeeded, you devil!" the Moon Man spat.

Bostiff swayed forward, raising Gil's automatic. The cripple needed only to squeeze a shot at the man who'd dared injure his master. At the same time, Angel, entering behind the ebony-robed Steve Thatcher, charged towards Doctor Satan. Here was the man who'd forced him to attack and almost kill his best friend!

Bostiff's movement put him in a direct line between the ex-pug and Satan. Unable to stop, Dargan plowed into the cripple like a line-backer defending a three-point lead. The shot meant for Steve Thatcher's heart went wild, ricocheted off the ceiling, and struck the unmoving Gil McEwen high in the shoulder.

The shock and burning pain broke the Lieutenant's paralysis spell. Dargan was on the floor before him, frantically trying to pin Bostiff down. In spite of the pain, McEwen joined the fray. He gave no thought to the fact that he was aiding two men he'd sworn to send to the electric chair.

With his good hand, McEwen grasped the would-be killer's gun-arm. He twisted that limb back nearly double. The arm was close to breaking when Bostiff's weapon clattered harmlessly to the floor.

From the doorway where she'd stopped after coming up behind Dargan, Sue McEwen shouted, "Moon Man! Satan is getting away!"

A false panel opened in what appeared to be a solid wall of complex machinery. Beyond it lay a dark and narrow passageway.

"You think you're clever, Detective Steve Thatcher," Hell's messenger called as the panel swung shut behind him. "But Doctor Satan always has an edge."

Then the panel sealed tightly. Not even Ned Dargan's mighty muscles could reopen it.

"Steve?" repeated Gil. His voice was oddly weak. "Steve Thatcher - my daughter's fiance - the Moon Man?"

"No, dad!" came Sue's quick denial. "It's another of that devil's lies!"

But the seed had been planted. McEwen wanted to disbelieve Doctor Satan's parting shot, but he was a good and thorough detective. His obsession with the mysterious thief who plagued Great City would not allow him to overlook any possibility, however distasteful. Steve's thumbprint would be matched against one known definitely to belong to the Moon Man. The truth would then be inescapable.

Steve Thatcher did not waste time reflecting on the consequences of that event now. Distressing as they were, there was nothing he could do, and there were still Satan and his lackey to take care of. Bostiff had taken advantage of Gil's numbed shock to break loose from him and Dargan. With a speed belied by his mutilated shape, he shot down another passageway and up the narrow staircase at its end.

"Stay here with Sue and her father, Angel," the Moon Man ordered. "In case Doctor Satan comes back. I'm going after that refugee from a freak show!"

CHAPTER [28]
SATAN'S BLOOD

"Y ou can't yet," insisted Beatrice Dale. "You're not fully recovered."
Ascott Keane forced his long legs to stand erect, in spite of his secretary's protests.

"I'm well enough," he replied, his eyebrows drawing down into heavy, straight black lines over his light gray eyes. "Didn't you see him? Doctor Satan just raced past, without giving us a second glance! He looked like he was wounded! If I'm ever to put an end to his menace, it must be now!"

"With an athlete's swiftness, Keane sprang down along the same corridor his arch foe followed. The passage ended in a steep and twisting stairway. Keane clambered up in pursuit. After a half dozen steps he had to catch at the stone walls with his long, powerful fingers to keep from falling. He'd slipped on a wet spot. The sleuth touched a finger to the dark, moist patch, licked the tip with his tongue.

"Satan's blood," he whispered, excited. His gray eyes glittered ecstatically. "He **is** wounded!"

No Keane vaulted the steps two and three at a time. At the end of his treacherous climb he found a creaking door which flapped open and shut, open and shut...

Wind whipped across the castle's roof, striking Keane in the face like a blow from a fist. What the criminologist saw, on the opposite side of that flat expanse, would have frozen most men's limbs with astonishment. But Keane was used to the unexpected, where Satan was concerned.

His red robes flapping, the enemy of mankind was climbing into the gondola of an enormous balloon. The great gray airship had been hidden from sight from the ground by the tall castle battlements. The sound of the roof door slamming fully open caused Satan to pause in his flight. He turned his head and, seeing Keane, cursed bitterly the man who'd dogged his trail almost since his career began. Fear and hatred glared uncontrollably in the coal-black eyes all but hidden by the mask of scarlet.

"I haven't time for you now, Keane!" Satan cried. "But I make you this promise: the next time our paths cross, you shall die!"

A knife flashed silver in the sinister figure's hand. With a desperate urgency, Satan hacked at the single thick mooring rope.

"Master!" came a plaintive cry from another corner off the roof. "Don't leave without faithful Bostiff!"

So the roof had more than one entrance, thought Keane. But

Satan would not jeopardize his own safety for even the loyalest of his assistants. The mystic pushed his broad-shouldered body and powerful legs to the utmost.

The mooring rope parted with a jarring shock. Keane's hands grasped the lip of the gondola in a final burst of effort. His arms stretched to their limits. With perfect muscular coordination, he hauled himself aboard. Satan sent out a mental impulse, trying to control Keane's mind, but the sleuth was too well shielded. In a rashly futile bid to do away with his adversary, Satan hurled his knife. The pain of his wounded hand - an injury that would never have happened if he'd not been so totally taken by surprise - ruined his aim. The weapon whizzed past Keane's lean face, missing by a wide margin.

Satan then reached into the folds of his cloak to withdraw a green capsule. This was his last weapon. But Keane was upon him before he could bring it into play. The amateur detective clutched at the fiend's throat, his fingers reaching under the devil mask. Keane wanted with all his heart to choke the life from the master of evil.

"Before you die," Keane gasped as his free hand reached for the red cloth mask, "I'll see who you really are!"

"NO!" screamed Satan. "No man sees the face of Doctor Satan and lives to tell of it!" With Keane's knee pinning his arm, Satan could not shatter the green capsule against his opponent. He had to free the hand which held the arcane device. Craftily, Satan shifted his weight.

"No, you don't!" Keane countered. His hand left the mask to snatch Satan's wrist. So tight was that grip, Satan could not retain the capsule in his numbed fingers. Neither could he give Keane a chance to use it against him. With a twist of his thumb, the man in red tossed the capsule out of the gondola.

The sinister weapon smashed on the rooftop, within a foot of Bostiff's pleading form. There was a bubbling hiss when it struck; where it touched, the stone melted through to the room below.

"No, Master!" the piteous creature shouted, thinking the device had been deliberately hurled. "It's me! Bostiff!"

The Moon Man, following close behind the hideous cripple, assumed the deadly capsule was meant for a different target - himself. With the practiced aim of a Great City Police top marksman, Thatcher returned the attack. He fired his automatic at Satan's escape vehicle, unaware that Keane was also aboard.

The men in the gondola struggled fiercely, each grappling for the other's throat. Steve's bullet flew harmlessly over their heads, finding its mark in the gas-inflated balloon.

A fearful explosion rent the air. Flames shot out, consuming the delicate fabric of the airship. The gondola began sinking to a fiery death. By this time the wind had carried it out over the edge of the rooftop, so that the flaming contraption was drifting towards Murder River. It has just dropped beneath a cornice when Ascott Keane made his frantic leap from the vehicle of doom.

Long, strong fingers dug desperately for a hand hold in the crumbling stone. The Moon Man hurried to his aid. As the sphere-headed criminal pulled the supernatural sleuth to safety, a blood-chilling scream echoed from below.

"Satan's death cry," Thatcher observed.

"Let us pray that it is," added Keane.

"Look out!"

Beatrice Dale had hurried after her employer, reaching the roof top in time to see his narrow escape. Her warning cry alerted the two men to the still active menace of Bostiff. The cripple was hitching himself toward the pair of sleuths at a fantastic speed. Steve raised his gun. The creature's dull eyes seemed unaware of the threat as he swung past the two men.

"Master!" croaked his cruel, misshapen mouth. "Wait for me!"

The cripple did not even pause at the brink of the roof. His momentum hurdled him off the edge to plunge into the cold, murky depths of the river below, following the man his twisted mind worshipped... a man perfectly willing to let his misshapen aide suffer death or capture at the hands of the Great City police, the Moon Man, and the near-fanatic Ascott Keane.

CHAPTER [29]
RESOLUTION

"**...IBN** *abeth hali tun.*"

Ascott Keane intoned the final mystic words of his spell. He removed his lightly-touching finger from Gil McEwen's forehead.

"It is done," he stated.

Steve Thatcher looked down at the peaceful sleeping form of his future father-in-law. He'd long since removed his hinged helmet. Concern showed plainly on his face.

"He will remember nothing of Doctor Satan's accusation?" the detective sergeant asked.

"Blocking that specific memory was child's play. He could have uncovered your identity any number of times in the past, Steve, just by pressing a bit harder. But he would not admit the possibility to himself. McEwen's own subconscious has worked to protect your secret, and will continue to do so if you don't get careless."

"I don't intend to," Steve replied. "You've known all along, haven't you? You've read my mind."

Keane shook his head. "There was no need for that. When we were first introduced, outside the kennels, I noticed a layer of soot on your shoes... soot that you could only have collected by being inside the house!"

Thatcher grinned. "And I thought I was a good detective!"

"You are Steve. Which is why your disguise and criminal activities puzzle me. Satan was a human devil, committing crimes for the sake of thrills, adopting his bizarre costume because it amused him to emulate the Prince of Darkness. But you're a level-headed fellow. Why the charade?"

"It's difficult to explain, Ascott. I like to think that the Moon Man brings some measure of light, however feeble, to the thousands of people suffering in the black night of poverty. I only steal from those who can well afford the loss, disposing of the gains to those who cannot live without it. Angel can tell you that."

Keane's eyes narrowed to two gray glints, staring down along his high-bridged, patrician nose at the earnest young detective.

"Yes," Keane said, "I do understand. There are depths within you, Steve Thatcher, which even you do not suspect. I do not approve of your methods, but neither can I fault your goals.

We all must fight evil in our own ways."

Keane extended a long-fingered hand. Steve gripped it in a firm handshake.

"Now you and Angel had better leave," Keane continued. "The Lieutenant will waken shortly. With the end of Doctor Satan's threat to Great City, I fear your shaky truce is also over."

Steve nodded. He gave Sue, standing over her father, a long and tender kiss. Then once more the mysterious Argus helmet enclosed his features.

"See you later, honey," he said.

Angel came up behind his friend. "Say, Boss," he said, "don't you think we better get a squad up here?"

"We'll stop at a phone booth on the way back to the city, Angel. It might be a good idea for Steve Thatcher to join that squad."

Black robes flapping, the Moon Man and his emissary left.

Beatrice Dale breathed a deep sigh of relief.

"It's finally over, Ascott," she said, gently massaging his neck with her long, slim fingers. Her eyes glowed with a light which Keane, for all his sleuthing ability, had never yet really observed. "We can begin leading normal lives. Doctor Satan is destroyed."

"Is he?" Keane mused. "Can it be this easy?"

Ascott Keane'd doubts lingered and grew. Police went through the castle inch by inch, yet no clue to the fiend's real identity was found; Keane expected as much. A team of scientific experts studied the remnants of the Sonar Ray and other strange equipment abandoned by the man in the devil mask. They could neither reconstruct it nor discover how it worked. Keane expected that, too, considering it a boon.

The river patrol discovered the charred remains of the gondola and fragments of burnt balloon cloth washed ashore within a half mile of the looming cliff side. Thorough dredging operations were inaugurated. No bodies were recovered. Ascott Keane had both expected and feared as much. Murder River had been known to carry large objects, including corpses, all the way to the sea. That fact little reassured the sleuth.

At a point two and a quarter miles from the site Huntington's Folly, well outside the radius of the police search, a pair of ragged figures pulled themselves from the river's deadly currents. One was a tall man, imposing

"Doctor Satan will be avenged!"

even dressed in tattered rags of scarlet. His first action, on reaching the safety of the riverbank, was to reach anxiously for his face.

Satisfied, he relaxed. The mask was still in place, held there by the sturdy skull-cap.

The figure accompanying him was grotesque, a legless man whose great, gorilla-like head was set on tremendous shoulders, as high as a normal man's waist. He swayed back and forth, shaking off droplets of water, supporting his gigantic torso on hands calloused from doubling as feet.

"Again," the tall man muttered darkly. "Again, Ascott Keane has thwarted my plans to rule the world through terror. Very well, Keane. Now I will carry the battle directly to your doorstep! Doctor Satan will be avenged!"

"Yes, Master," croaked the crippled Bostiff in concord. "Vengeance for us both!"

THE END

FURY IN VERMONT

By Ron Fortier

T he silver painted 812 Cord Cabriolet wound its way smoothly over the small back roads of Vermont's northern woods like a sparkling needle through an evergreen haystack. The V-8 Lycoming engine, with its horizontal supercharger, purred like a contented lioness on the hunt. The canvas top had been sealed in its rear compartment and the two occupants relished the cool air of a late summer morning.

They were a striking couple to say the least. The man in the passenger seat was a tall, lanky fellow with thick brown hair the color of rich loam. He had a tanned complexion that testified to an outdoor life further enhanced by the weathered crow's feet around his energetic green eyes. Decked out in heavy boots, jeans, a cotton shirt and leather jacket, Donat Cartier was a dramatic, handsome figure.

When people learned he had once worn the bright red jacket of a Canadian Royal Mounted policeman, they accepted the declaration immediately. This was clearly a man to with reckon with. Now, as the wind whipped over his face and right shoulder, Cartier mused inwardly about that old career. Had it not been for the incident in Manitoba four years earlier, he might still be manhunter in the frozen north-country.

He might also be dead, which would have been his fate but for the timely intervention of the beautiful woman behind the wheel of the speeding auto. He looked at her and marveled for the thousandth time at the stunning feminine perfection of his companion.

With a tall, blonde Scandinavian mother and a Japanese father, Kate Furyaka was a stunning creature. At six feet, she had not only inherited her athlete mother's height, but also her voluptuousness. Whereas her dusky skin and shoulder length raven black hair gave her a truly exotic appearance. Her dazzling blue eyes gave a faint almond shape hint to her oriental heritage while her full red lips were uniquely her own.

Fury, as the world press had come to call her, was attired in her normal traveling suit consisting of calf-high leather boots, jodhpurs, a wide utility belt festooned with pouches and a light blue, heavy cotton shirt, the sleeves rolled up past her elbows. Not one to flout her good looks, she had no need of garish make up or gaudy jewelry. Her only concession to either

93

was a thin veneer of lipstick and a single gold pendant draped around her long neck with the Egyptian ankh symbol upon it. There was also a man's wristwatch on her left arm and she wore soft leather racing gloves.

"So, Kate, tell me again why we are traipsing through the backwoods of cow and cheese country on such a lovely day?"

Without taking her eyes from the winding road, Fury replied. "Okay, but try to pay attention this time."

Cartier winced. "Hey, I was partying last night. How'd I know you were going to come knocking at my door at the crack of dawn." He massaged his temple as if rubbing away a headache. "You could at least have brought along a pot of coffee."

"In the glove compartment," Fury offered. "Sorry I couldn't stop to get doughnuts. But they're really not good for you."

Cartier opened the compartment and pulled out the orange colored Thermos and began to unscrew the cap. "What's the point, in our line of work; you don't really expect to die of old age, do you?" He began to pour the steaming black coffee into the cup-top. "You want some?"

"No thanks. Maybe later, when we get to Cherryfield."

"Now that's a pretty name. No doubt for a quaint little New England hamlet." He raised his cup to her in salute, and then took a tentative sip. "Ah, the elixir of renewal."

"A month ago I ran into my old college professor, Doctor Ann Wilkerson. She's a social anthropologist doing work on secret cults in western civilization. During lunch together, she told me she'd been following a series of bizarre news stories from this part of country."

"What kind of stories?"

"People disappearing in the woods. Experienced hikers and vacationers. At least six in the past three months. After extensive search parties failed to locate any of the missing, the authorities pretty much just closed the book on the entire matter."

"But not your friend, the doc?"

"No. Apparently she had gotten a letter from a Forest Ranger alluding to some kind of satanic cult operating within the area."

"Aha, now the plot thickens. Did your friend contact this guy?"

"Oh yes. Turns out he was the last person to vanish."

"That's decidedly not good."

Fury gripped the steering wheel tightly as she navigated a particularly sharp turn that took led them to a down sloping stretch along a small valley brook to their left. The Cord hugged the road like a magnet on wheels.

"Ann said she was going to come here and investigate. Starting from the place where the Ranger's letter was postmarked."

"Cherryfield, Vermont."

"Check. Last night I got a call for her assistant, frantic with worry. Ann usually checks in with her office every few days. Only now it's been five days since her last call and they are getting worried something has happened to her."

"That does not sound good at all, *mon ami*." Cartier had a habit of slipping back into his native French when his thoughts sobered. Fury took it as a good sign.

What was most definitely not a good sign was the black and white police car parked diagonally across the road as Fury came around another hairpin turn at a better than average speed. Slapping one foot down on the clutch and the other on the brake pedal, she jerked the stick and downshifted hard into second gear to bring the car under control and stop it quick. The back tires screeched in protest, but the brakes did their job and even with a slight slant to the front end, they came to a complete halt a good thirty yards away from the blocking black and white cruiser.

"Now what the hell is going on?" Cartier spat out, still gripping the walnut dashboard. Fortunately he'd resealed the thermos before it bounced off his lap and hit the floor.

Fury switched off the engine and sat back into her cushioned seat, her tensed muscles relaxing.

The door to the police sedan popped open and a beefy deputy sheriff climbed out with a cold smile on his round, chubby face. He tilted his visored cap back on his head, hitched up his gun belt and sauntered over to the Cord.

"Hi yah, folks. That was some nice driving, lady. Way you stopped your car like that, on the dime."

"Well, you did surprise us," Fury said cordially. "Is there some kind of problem ahead?"

The deputy answered with a question. "Where you folks headed?"

"Cheeryfield. Our map says it's up ahead."

"Oh, yeah. That it is, ma'am. But I'm afraid I can't let you pass. You see we've got us a smallpox outbreak and the state medical people have put the whole town on quarantine."

"Really? Funny I didn't see anything about that in the papers."

"Well, that's because it only happened a few days ago now."

"I see."

"So, like I said, you're going to have to turn around and go back the way you came. Sorry."

"I'm sure you are only doing your duty, officer. But might I have a look at your quarantine certificate."

"Huh?" the big man blinked, clearly unprepared for her question. "You mean like papers?"

"Yes," Fury smiled innocently. "You can't establish a legal quarantine without the proper authority from the department of health and safety. You should have one in your possession or your blockade of a public thoroughfare is illegal."

"Hey, are you some kind of lawyer or something?"

"No, but I am aware of the laws, officer. Do you have such a certificate?"

The deputy took a step back from the door and slowly dropped his right hand over his gun butt. His foolish grin had been replaced with one of obvious aggravation. At the same time, Fury felt the medallion on her skin heat up. A gift from Chandu, the famed magician, the ankh was in reality a protective talisman that warned her when supernatural forces were present.

"I ain't got time for this, lady. I told you the town was off limits. Now I want you and your friend to turn this car around and skeedaddle."

Fury scrutinized the man's face more intently and began to sense the threat radiating from him.

"Is that clear enough for you?"

"Very." Fury threw the door open hard and it slammed into the deputy just as the gun in his hand was clearing its holster. The impact jarred him enough to make him drop the weapon and fall back stumbling.

Then he stopped and snapped his head up and strange transformation masked his features. Suddenly his eyes were blood red and his skin took on a coarse, green hue.

"Bitch!" The voice coming from his throat was inhuman. "Now I will rip out your heart and eat it raw." The hand he raised up was gnarled and the nails extended like claws.

"He's possessed!" Fury declared, turning to her companion. "He means to kill us!"

Not one to waste time with explanations, Cartier rose up out of his seat, climbed over the windshield onto the hood and then dove onto the changeling. The two went down in a heap of kicking legs and swinging fists. Around and around on the hard-packed ground they rolled, each trying to gain an advantage over the other.

As if testifying to his abnormal nature, the rotund deputy was clearly holding his own against the taller, more powerful Cartier. Spitting and snarling like a cornered beast, the man-monster finally threw off his advisory and vaulted back to his feet. Standing like a growling gorilla, hands down by his side, he shambled over to the fallen Canadian and picked him up by the scruff of the neck. With an effortless heave, he yanked the startled Cartier into the air, holding him over his head as if he were a rag doll.

"First I'm going to crush your boyfriend," he yelled, his tongue appearing forked and black in his mouth. "And then I'm coming for you, bitch!"

Fury, who had come out of the car and watched the contest by the open driver's door, now took action. She tapped a panel on the door's interior and instantly it slid out to reveal a platinum plated Colt .45 automatic with an extended barrel. It was in her right hand in a clean, practiced motion and then leveled at the demonic deputy.

"I don't think so!" Fury corrected at the same time she pulled the trigger and pumped three quick rounds into the thing's chest. Each steel jacketed bullet tore through its torso and came out the backside with chunks of flesh and gore and a huge spray of blood. With each lethal discharge, the gun produced a deafening boom that echoed through the still air around them. Fury had to fight to hold the barrel steady. The monster's legs buckled and it dropped Cartier, who fell on his side and rolled away.

"Arghh!" cried the wounded menace as he lunged for Fury. She fired another two shots a point blank range. The first went through his throat and the second found its mark between the creature's eyes and exited out the back of his head. He made a gurgling noise, blood gushed out his mouth and then he fell over face first into the dirt at her feet.

The thing shuddered violently and then was still.

"What the hell kind of nightmare was that thing?" Cartier asked, coming to his feet. He approached it cautiously, slapping dirt and grass off his jacket.

"I'm not sure," Fury replied, moving around the dead body. "But I've got some ideas."

"So what do we do now?"

Fury lowered her gun, smoke thinning from the long barrel. "We put this thing in the trunk of the cruiser and then drive it off the road where it won't be found for a while."

"Okay. Then what?"

"Then," Fury smile, turning her eyes to the road beyond the police vehicle. "We go to Cheeryfield."

***

"I don't think so!"

It was shortly after high noon when they rolled into the business center of the picturesque township of Cheeryfield. Rolling down the lane between historic old buildings of commerce, Fury and Cartier were hard pressed to believe there existed a malevolent secret in this rustic setting. Massive oaks and elms lined the street to either side, providing ample shade for the shops like the Handy Hardware and the Main St. General Store.

Across from the Town Hall and Post Office building they came upon a restaurant featuring a sign that read, POT LUCK HEAVEN. As there were several empty spaces before it, Fury pulled up and parked.

"So, what do you say, Donat? This looks as good a place as any to start." They both climbed out of the car and stretched their limbs before starting up the three steps to the eatery's front door.

"And while we're at it, let's grab a bite," Cartier suggested, as he pulled the door open in a gentlemanly fashion to allow her to enter. "I'm so hungry, I could eat a horse."

"Okay, but questions first. Food second."

The interior of the Pot Luck was open, airy and friendly looking. Dozens of round, wooden tables were scattered to either side of the long, rectangular room and Fury estimated some twenty-odd souls were enjoying lunch. To their front was a long bar were other locals, most in dungarees and farm boots, were filling their bellies with what smelled like delicious, well prepared fare.

The small reindeer bell over the front door announced their presence, the buzz of conversations abruptly ceased to be replaced by an awkward, cold silence and multiple heads turned in their direction.

"Oh yeah," Cartier whispered behind Fury's ear. "They really seem like a friendly bunch."

A middle aged woman with her hair in a bun and pencil sticking out her barrette came around the cash register, wiping her hands with her red and white checkered apron. The nametag on her blouse told them she was Gladys.

"Hi, folks. Don't mind the stares. We just don't get too many visitors up here in the woods, is all.

"My name is Gladys. I own the place. Would you like a nice table by one of the windows?"

Fury started to reach into her hip pocket to produce the picture of her friend, Doctor Ann Wilkerson.

"That would be fine, but first, my name is Kate..."

"I know you!" blurted an excited, high pitched voice. Attached to it, coming out of the swinging doors to the rear kitchen, was a lovely young girl, also in a waitress uniform and carrying a tray with hot entrees. She was a younger version of the hostess.

Gladys turned from her customers to the freckled faced employee. "Dana?"

"You're that famous explorer that travels all around the world in your own airship. Right?" The girl's big brown eyes looked like they were going to come out of her head.

"Yes," Fury acknowledged politely. "It's called the Valkerie."

"Miss Fury!" Dana said, looking at her mother. "You remember, Ma, I read you the article a while back. They found that lost island in the South Pacific filled with those old type monsters on it."

"They're called dinosaurs," Cartier offered gladly. "And you are one hundred percent right, sweetheart. This is none other than Katherine Gunnilla Furyaka herself. Or as you already pointed out, she whom the world's press has dubbed Miss Fury."

"Wow, I ain't never met a real celebrity before," the young woman confessed, while remaining frozen where she stood.

"And most likely you'll never meet another one if you don't get about your work and get those specials to the Anderson table." Gladys was clearly bemused by her daughter's foolishness. "People get their food cold; it's not going to be good for business."

Dana rolled her eyes at her mother. "Oh, Ma." But Gladys refused to acquiesce and the girl shuffled off.

Gladys indicated the empty table to their right. Fury and Cartier followed her lead and sat down. Seeing the menu standing against a napkin holder, he grabbed it and began studying what the establishment offered. Meanwhile Fury had produced the black and white snapshot and was holding it up.

"We are looking for a friend who was doing some work in this general area. This is her picture. I was wondering if you might have seen her in the past few weeks?"

Gladys took the photo and then nodded in recognition. "Oh, yes, the professor lady. I remember her."

"You do! She was here?"

"Yes. I believe it was about two weeks ago. She was all over town asking folks all kinds of questions about those poor souls that had gotten lost in the woods."

Cartier had put down the menu. Like Fury, he was now all ears.

"Would you know where she is at the moment?" Fury asked, fearing the reply.

"Sorry, miss." Gladys shook her head negatively and returned the picture. "I do know she was staying at the old Algonquin hotel down the road about a block. Then one day, just like that she was gone."

"Would you mind if I asked your customers if they might have seen her as well?"

"Are you saying she's missing too?"

"Yes, her office in New York hasn't heard from her in quite some time and that's why we're here."

"Gosh, that's really too bad. She was a really nice lady. Look, dear, why don't you give me your order. Then, while my husband, Ernie, is getting it made, I'll talk to the folks here for yah. Won't make them nervous that way, if you know what I mean."

Fury was only too glad to go along with Gladys's offer. She ordered a fried chicken plate, while Cartier ordered three hamburgers and a side order of French fries with a milk shake.

"Hey, I'm a growing boy," he grinned, holding up his hands palms out. The real truth was his unique metabolism, which Fury was all too familiar with. Donat Cartier, in the course of his unusual activities, tended to burn off more calories than an average man his age.

As they were sitting there, Dana came over with a pitcher of ice water and filled their glasses. She still looked at Fury with wonder and acted skittishly around her.

"You have a fan," Cartier observed, as Dana rushed off. Fury nodded and sipped her water.

Immediately she tasted the foreign drug. The tip of her tongue identified it as a sleep inducing powder. Her first instinct was to stop Cartier from gulping down his, but she realized the clear chemical would have no effect on his peculiar system. Instead, she slipped her right hand down to one of the small pouches on her belt, snapped it open and from it took a tiny white pill. Surreptitiously she put it her mouth, then took another swallow of the tainted water. The pill was a powerful antidote that would nullify the drug's effects instantly.

Forty minutes later the restaurant interlude had served only to refuel their stamina but brought them no closer to solving their mystery. As they left the Pot Luck and were returning to the Cord, a police coupe came rolling up the street at a reckless speed. It screeched to a stop behind the Cord's rear bumper and then ejected the big, hulking figure who'd been its driver. Dressed like the deputy they'd encountered on the road, this officer also had a star pinned to his breast pocket.

"I'm Sheriff Otis Claymore. Can I ask you folks how you got here?"

"Excuse me?" Fury's medallion began to warm. "How we got here?"

"Yes. Which way did you come into town by?"

Cartier, now standing beside Fury, pointed down the main drag. "From Route 12 out of Rutland. Why?"

"Did you see a deputy anywhere out there?" The man wasn't giving away any more than he had to. He had a pitted face, with a sharp roman nose and gray eyes that hinted at cruelty.

"No, we didn't." Cartier continued to be their spokesman. "Why, did you lose one?"

Sheriff Claymore's face hardened and Fury nudged Cartier slightly. "We didn't see anyone on the road, Sheriff. It was pretty much deserted all the way the last twenty miles of the main road."

"I see," Claymore eyed her with obvious suspicion. They both knew it was a lie. Then the look was replaced by one of surprised recognition.

"Do I know you? You look familiar."

"My name is Kate Fury, I've been in the papers a few times."

Kate extended her hand. Claymore ignored it.

"Right. Now I recall. You were mixed it up with some kind of Mexican vampires a while back."

"The papers tend to exaggerate. The government asked me to look into some border smuggling affair. That was all."

"So, what are you doing in Cherryfield?"

Fury hated his demeanor and for a second entertained the notion of being flippant ala Cartier. But the heat from her necklace had convinced her that the sheriff was as dangerous as his now deceased deputy. If she was to get to the heart of this mystery, she had to play along. She held up the photo of Ann Wilkerson.

"We're looking for this woman, she's a friend of mine."

"The professor from New York," Claymore sneered. "Yeah, she was here. Looking for devil worshippers or some such, as I recall."

"You spoke to her?"

"Only to tell her there was nothing like that around these parts. So she packed up her bags and left. That was about a week ago today."

Another lie. Fury wanted to throttle the truth out of him, but her common sense held firm. A quick and thoughtless act would serve no end and most likely jeopardize Wilkerson's life, if she were still among the living.

"Would you know where she was going when she left?" Fury hoped her performance was sincere and believable. "Her associates back home are really worried about her."

Claymore's face relaxed slightly, believing he was controlling the situation. "Don't really know. She did make some comments about going further up north into Quebec. But I can't swear to it."

"I see."

"If you like, I'll notify the feds in Burlington and put a missing persons report."

"That won't be necessary, Sheriff. If Ann...Doctor Wilkerson, is pursuing a lead, there's no telling where she'll end up."

"Sorry I couldn't be of more help."

"Not your fault, Sheriff. I think we'll take a room at the hotel." Claymore's eyes narrowed. Fury continued, "We've had a long day on the road."

"Well, the hotel is just around the corner."

"Yes, Gladys told us. Thank you, Sheriff."

Claymore touched the brim of his cap and nodded. "My pleasure, Miss Fury. You have a good day now."

With that, the big man got back into his cruiser and drove off. Fury and Cartier watched until he was gone from sight and then turned to one another.

"Is he one of..them?" Cartier asked. "You know, like that thing on the road."

Fury pulled open the driver's door to the Cord and answered.

"Oh yes. Indeed he is."

"So what the hell is going on around here?" Cartier questioned, going around the back end of the car.

"Let's get squared away at the hotel, and away from prying eyes," Fury said starting the engine. "Then I'll tell you what I do know. I think it's going to be an eventful night."

***

"They're all asleep!" Cartier proclaimed as he returned to Fury's hotel room in the Algonquin. It was eight o'clock, seven hours since they had checked in and taken adjoining rooms. Now she was seated in yoga position on the braided rug in front of the bed oiling her twin .45 automatics. The two custom made firearms were laid in pieces on a black cloth, with assorted cleaning rags and brushes.

"It's just like you said," Cartier went on, closing the door behind him and sitting down on the edge of the bed. "Everyone in the entire place is out like a light. The desk clerk and a few town folks in main lobby are all snoring away. Most likely in the same spot they were in when the sun set."

"And did you attempt to awaken any of them?" Fury picked up a long steel barrel and slid a pipe-brush through it.

"Yes, I did. Like you suggested, and sure enough none of them would come around. It was like they were all in comas?"

"They have been drugged."

"What? The whole town?"

"Yes. The agent is in their water supply. I tasted it back at the Pot Luck."

"You did? Why didn't you tell me?"

"Please, Donat. You know fully well you can't be drugged and as for myself, I easily countered the effects with one of the anti-toxin pills from my belt.

"I saw no need to alarm you."

"Gee, thanks." Cartier made a petulant face, then lay back on his bed, folding his hands behind his head on the plush pillows. "So who do you think is behind all this? Claymore?"

"It's a good bet," Fury agreed, beginning to deftly reassemble her powerful handguns. "My guess is he's part of a secret group that has managed to insinuate itself into the community and is now controlling it."

Cartier whistled. "Wow. For what purposes? Hey, maybe it's connected to those people disappearing?"

"That would be my guess." Fury turned her head around a indicated the darkening night outside the windows. "And if I'm not mistaken, we won't have to wait very long to discover what happens next."

She put away her cleaning kit, then stood and reached into her traveling bag. From it she took a leather harness and strapped it about her torso snugly. Then she slapped two clips into both pistols and slid them into their holsters tight against her ribs.

"We are going to put out the lights and let our mysterious adversaries think they have succeeded in putting us out of action."

Cartier sat up and looked at her with anticipation. "And then we see who comes calling."

"Exactly." The smile on Fury's face was deadly.

***

The sun's long journey through the summer skies ended dramatically as it set over the western mountains. The sentinel street lamps along Main Street sparked to life and offered staggered islands of light. The thick clouds kept the yellow half moon from offering any support. Still, it remained enough for Fury and Cartier to see by. At approximately ten fifteen p.m., cloaked draped figures began to appear from various buildings and make their way up the middle of the empty road.

They were a silent lot, keeping to themselves, their features hidden beneath their heavy thick cowls and their hands lost in voluminous sleeves.

As this eerie parade passed before the hotel, Fury and Cartier stepped back from the window so as not to be spotted.

"What now?" Cartier whispered, as though the marching figures below might have supernatural hearing.

Fury was about to reply when there was a creaking noise from the stairs at the end of the hallway. Fury put her finger up to her lips and indicated the closet behind her. Quickly the pair ducked into the small space and carefully closed the door to leave it ajar by a small fraction. Enough to witness what would happen next.

Footsteps shuffled along the corridor and then sound of a key inserted in the brass lock. There was a tense moment of silence and then soft creak of the door being swung inward.

Squeezed together, their line of sight limited to the seeing the bed and wall, they could not tell how many nocturnal visitors they actually had.

Then a small yellow flashlight beam appeared and played over the rumpled shape on the bed. Fury had carefully positioned the pillows and blankets to make it appear as if she were actually beneath them. Cartier had done the same. But would the ruse work? The couple held their breaths and Cartier went so far as to cross his fingers.

"She's out cold," spoke a raspy, harsh voice.

"So's the other one," came an answering male voice from across the hall. "Come on, let's go or will miss the gathering ceremonies."

Then, without further inspection, the door was shut and the footsteps retreated back the way they had come. Fury and Cartier bolted out of the closet.

"It worked, Kate!"

"Yes, but that was only the first part. Now we've got to catch them before they get too far! Hurry."

With as much care as the cloaked intruders, she pushed open the door and went out; Cartier was close on her heels. The pair opted to take the back stairs and exit the hotel via a door that led to a huge, tree covered yard. Silently they worked their way around the building to witness their visitors shuffling along the sidewalk in a hurried attempt to join their confederates.

Peering around the corner of the building, Fury could make out a least a dozen robed figures heading for the north end of the street. Several in the lead where holding up torches that cast an eerie ball of light about them.

She brought her head close to Cartier's and whispered, "It's time we joined the party."

He smiled in the moonlight and gave her a thumbs up signal.

Wasting no time, they went after the mysterious clan, hugging the store fronts where the awnings made the shadows deeper. Fury saw that the group ahead of them was taking a turn at the end of the road and moving off into the woods. She tapped Cartier's arm and jogged across the street.

Their one advantage lay in the fact that the two men who had come to check their status were a considerable distance from the main group. That gap was all Fury and her companion would need to attack.

As the stragglers started into the forest, Fury sprinted forward and tackled the end man. The two went down into the soft ground and before the fellow knew what had jumped him, Fury smashed his jaw with a hard judo palm strike. The man beneath her went limp.

At the same time, his partner had heard the scuffle and turned around, only to see Donat Cartier's fist filling his world. The next second he was seeing stars.

The two adventurers then dragged the unconscious men into the thickets, removed their hooded cloaks and donned them. Luckily the two sleeping fellows had been tall and their woolen garments fit Fury and Cartier perfectly. Fury would have liked to tie the men with their belts and make them secure, but with every second that passed, the others were going further up the wooded path into the surrounding hills.

There was nothing for it but to hope the two men were soundly out of commission for a long while. Lifting the voluminous folds of their cloaks, the duo raced into the trees after the dwindling torches. Within a few hundred yards, they caught up and fell into step behind the marching cultists.

As they wound their way up the rising slope, they went deeper into the rugged, hill country. Fury and Cartier maintained the pace with no difficulties, each of them in top physical condition. Finally the group arrived at a jagged outcrop of massive granite boulders. Hidden amidst this cluster of hard rocks was the opening maw of an ominous cave. The torch bearers continued onward into its hidden depths.

The wide, natural tunnel was lit by more brands affixed to the rock walls by steel braces. The air around them was cool and damp. The smell of decaying mold offended their nostrils.

Then, as they went further into the bowels of the mountain, they heard the rhythmic beating of loud drums. The loudness of the banging swelled the closer they approached its subterranean source.

The group reached a huge cavern that had been cut from the earth like a natural amphitheater. It was as wide across as several football fields and the ceiling reminded Fury of the many church interiors she had visited in her travels. There were small, flittering objects darting about overhead and she assumed they were bats, annoyed by the commotion of drums and the intrusion of the robed assembly.

At the center of the huge arena stood a wooden platform on which sat two members of the secret sect. Before them were large, round African drums which they beat incessantly with thick, polished sticks. Behind these men were small openings to connecting tunnels. Fury imagined the area was honeycombed with dozens of them. To either side of the wide stage, were barrels filled with burning coal. The flames from these two cans both provided light and a small degree of warmth in the dank atmosphere. The black, oily tendrils of smoke wafted away into the outlying tunnel branches.

As the group of robed men bunched together in front of the raised platform, a single figure appeared from the cave and to the left of it. Draped in a red cassock and cowl, the mysterious player walked up the two stairs and strode confidently to the stage's center. There he threw back his hood and raised his arms high in the air.

"Brethren," Sheriff Otis Claymore called out. "The time has come to call forth the God Yoteth. To do it homage. To offer our holy and wondrous sacrifice!"

The audience of true believers cheered and Fury and Cartier steeled themselves for whatever came next.

"Once again we have been blessed, my brothers." As he spoke, Claymore paced back and forth so that all in the vast cavern might hear his voice clearly. "One who is our enemy has been delivered to us and will now serve our master and his hunger."

Flames from the twin barrels were reflected in the man's eyes as he spun around and cried out towards the tunnel from which he had made his entrance. "Bring out the sacrifice to Yoteth and prepare for the summoning."

At this, two members of the green cloaked brotherhood appeared dragging with them a struggling, half naked female.

She was a short, auburn haired woman of middle age and her hands were bound in front of her with chains. A gag had been tied about her head to stifle her cries and she was attired only in her under garments, now soiled and torn. There were livid bruises and multiple cuts all over her exposed arms and legs. Fury recognized her friend, Ann Wilkerson immediately and had to restrain Cartier when he started to take a step forward.

"Wait," she whispered. "We need to know what we are facing, before we move."

Cartier concurred, but with obvious reservations. An old fashioned chauvinist, seeing a woman so savagely mistreated went against everything he believed in. He wanted nothing more than to rescue the abused professor and pummel her captors.

Once on the wooden floor, the two ruffians pulled their struggling prisoner to Claymore. He in turn, pointed to a man standing in the far corner next to a hand driven mechanical wench. At the leader's cue, this fellow began cranking the heavy wheel that controlled a massive cable suspended high in the crevices of the cavern's ceiling. Descending between massive stalactites, the cable dropped into the view over the heads Claymore and the kidnapped woman. At the end of the thick line was a heavy, iron hook. As it came within a few feet of his head, Claymore reached up and snagged hold of it. Then, he nodded to the two guards and they grasped the frantic woman and together raised her arms into the air. Claymore quickly slipped the hook under her wrist chains and the men released her weight. The frightened professor dangled a foot off the platform, her body twisting about in an vain attempt to free itself.

Seeing the smug look on the sheriff's face, Wilkerson suddenly stopped her gyrations and brought her feet up in an effort to kick his leering face. Claymore was slow to react and her left foot connected with his chest, hitting him hard and propelling him backwards.

"Bitch!" He regained his balance and composure, then looked to his loyal followers. "It is time. Come forth Yoteth, the white worm!"

Without missing a beat, the instrumentalists carried their drums off to either side of the stage and began pounding them harder and faster. At the same time, the assembly, with Claymore's lead, began an eerie chant.

"Yog Yoteth..rise up! Yog Yoteth we call on you from the bowels of hell!" Over and over, repeating each line, the gathering sang the words, at times almost drowning out the booming drums.

Fury felt a subtle change in the air around her akin to charged particles before a summer thunder storm. Something with the power to affect nature was coming nearer with each bang of the leather-covered drums. Cartier felt it too and pointed to the darkness directly behind the mock stage. A vague outline of a grayish shape was slowly materializing before their astonished eyes.

It was a monstrous worm, clearly six feet in height with a long, undulating body the size of a small bus. As it dragged itself into the light of the cavern, Fury was able to better discern its make up. The skin, made up of rubbery looking scales, wasn't gray but a dead, putrid white. It was not so much a hue as the lack of any such. As if the being's physical shape was devoid of any natural characteristics. But what clearly defined its alien nature was its head, an ugly, flat surface around which dozens of twisting, snake like tendrils grew. Each, long, finger ended at a red colored mouth filled with sharp teeth. At the middle of the eyeless face was its mouth, a gaping

hole from which a black, forked tongue jutted in and out as if the creature was in the throes of hunger.

It was. Hungry for the flesh of the suspended sacrificial offering Claymore had provided. As it came closer, the monstrosity reared up on its midsection to survey the cavern and its scenario awaiting it. A foul, sour odor radiated from its obscene shape as it shimmied nearer to the stage.

Claymore gave a hand sign and the two drummers stopped their banging. He was still on the stage near the helpless victim who was now transfixed by the sight of the pale, giant serpentine nightmare coming for her.

"See, oh master, the sacrifice of living flesh and blood we have prepared in accordance to the ancient ways. Now come, feast and give us your blessings."

"Actually," Fury called out, instantly getting Claymore's stunned attention. "I think that will be more than enough of this madness." With that, she threw off her cloak disguise and, in one fluid motion, whipped out her deadly .45s. All those around her took a startled step back, caught flatfooted by her surprise appearance.

"You!" Claymore screamed pointing at her like an outraged teacher whose lecture had been interrupted by some prankish child. "How dare you interfere with the rites of Yog Yoteth."

"Oh, I plan on doing lots more than that," Fury called back, warily keeping people away by waving her pistols about threateningly. She knew that wouldn't last long. Luckily, no one had noticed Cartier had moved off to the corner by the wench operator. He was now in position to play his part when Fury gave the command.

One of the brotherhood suddenly charged her and at point blank range, Fury shot him in the chest. The custom-made cartridge ripped a fist size hole through the man and threw him into the air to land in the arms of his outraged brethren. They managed to keep their anger in check. For the moment.

"You are out of your element here, Miss Fury!" Claymore reasoned. "Your bullets may inflict some damage on us, but they cannot harm the master."

"Which is why I brought along my friend." At that Cartier, rushed the man at the steel crank and knocked him cold with a hard right cross. Then, before anyone could react, he unlocked the wheel mechanism and lowered Doctor Wilkerson to her feet.

"Stop him!" Claymore commanded. As three of the secret society started for the Canadian, he looked to his gun toting mistress.

"Now, *mon cheri*?"

"Yes, now!" she yelled back.

Cartier proceeded to remove his own cloak and cowl. Then he kicked off his heavy boots and began unbuttoning his shirt. The trio approaching him stopped, confounded by his sudden striptease.

"Your friend is out of his mind!" Claymore laughed. "This is how you plan to defeat the great Yog Yoteth? With a naked man?"

"Actually it is not the man you have to worry about!"

Fury kept her guns poised against the mob surrounding her. Thanks to her height, she could see Cartier was now down to his boxer shorts and his virile torso was exposed for all to see. At its center, over his breast bone was a tattoo of a five pointed pentagram. Fury closed her eyes for a quick prayer, then spoke the words that would transform her friend into a creature of lore known the world over.

"*When the wolf cries in the night, man lays naked in the straw, then by the stars and the moon, there arises fang and claw.*"

She could feel the heat of her amulet as Cartier suddenly screamed out in gut-wrenching agony. His entire body began to convulse and change.

Coarse, russet brown hair erupted through his skin until his body was covered head to toe. His body arched in metamorphosis as his legs became longer and thinner at the same time his chest seemed to thicken and his nails and fingers extended into four inch claws. His once handsome face was lost behind the newly sprouted hair and his long, aquiline nose became an ugly, stunted snout. His mouth stretched and when he opened it, jagged fangs protruded; each dripping yellow saliva.

"AROOO!" the werewolf cried out as it fell on the three men unlucky enough to be within its reach. Claws swiped out and tore the weaker flesh asunder with beastly abandon.

"KILL THEM!" Claymore finally gasped, sensing for the first time the real threat of this new, supernatural foe. But he had waited too long.

As the men around Fury moved in, she began firing directly into them as she pirouetted about so none could take her from behind. The big automatics boomed in an ear-shattering cacophony that filled the chamber. Body after robed body was sent kicking into the air, chunks of anatomy blown away. Gunpowder flames spit from her twin barrels with vicious accuracy, never once missing a single shot.

Several of her attackers were of the same demon breed as the deputy on the highway. After that initial encounter, Fury had taken the extra precaution to coat her bullets with holy water, while loading her clips in the hotel earlier. She always kept an ounce flask in one of the pouches of her faceted utility belt. Thus, even though several of these combatants managed to reach her, that was as far as they got. Once shot, they went down and stayed down.

At the same time, the obscene slug had halted its progress toward the platform and was thrashing about in frustration. It could smell the carnage Fury and her transformed companion were inflicting and was confused. Normally such destruction was meant solely for its evil benefit but not now. Then the werewolf leaped onto the stage and confronted the hell spawn. Covered in blood and gore, the hairy, snarling wolfman flared his nostrils at the sight of the giant worm, instinctively knowing this was its real target.

The demon-worm knew fear.

Sensing that fear, the werewolf attacked.

As the two inhuman creatures collided, Sheriff Claymore tore at his own cumbersome robe to get at his own gun holster. Watching the werewolf tearing out chunks of Yog Yoteth's hide, the fanatical worshipper was desperate to save his foul master.

"NOOOO!" he bellowed, as the .38 Police Special appeared in his right hand. "You will not defile the master!"

But the werebeast was oblivious to the man's cries, his bloodlust having flooded all reason from his mind. As the monster worm thrashed about, its tentacle wrapping around one of Cartier's legs, he howled in pain. In retaliation, he gripped the tentacle with his claws and ripped it from the nightmare head. Yoteth spewed forth black blood, its gyrations increasing in intensity as the living nightmare was unfamiliar with pain.

Emboldened by the worm's distress, the werewolf continued to attack its soft, vulnerable hide with renewed savagery.

Fury, having decimated nearly half the brotherhood, was marginally aware of what was happening on the platform. The cavern floor was littered with her victims. When the pistol in her right hand clicked empty, there were only four robed cultist still on their feet. Limbs they used to good advantage by running pell-mell for the nearest exits in a final retreat to save their tainted lives.

Stray strands of black hair plastered Fury's forehead as she swiveled around in time to see Claymore aiming his pistol at Cartier, locked in a death struggle with Yoteth.

A better shot with her right hand, Fury, spinning about, threw both pistols into air, as she had been taught by cowboy film star, Tom Mix. The still loaded gun now in her right, she snapped her arm and fired. Her bullet caught Claymore in the back of the head, taking off most of his skull. Doctor Wilkerson screamed and watched in disgust as her would-be torturer crumbled at her feet.

Fury raced to the altar, holstered her pistols and vaulted onto the stage. Within seconds she had her friend off the dangling hook and chain and then, using a magician's trick, deftly unclasped her manacles. All the while the emaciated and grime-covered woman kept staring at her in disbelief, as if she were a ghost.

"Ann, it's me, Kate."

"Oh, Kate!" Wilkerson collapsed in Fury's arms.

"It's alright, Ann," the lovely avenger soothed. "It's over now. You're safe."

The woman began to sob, her body shaking uncontrollably as the experience of her captivity finally unleashed itself on her psyche. Fury held her tightly, patting her shoulders and mouthing words of encouragement. She knew her friend was a strong soul and sure enough, within minutes, Dr. Ann Wilkerson stepped out of her embrace, looked up at her face and gave her a lopsided smile.

"Thank you, Kate. I knew you'd come and find me."

"That's what friends are for," Fury acknowledged. "You'd have done the same for me."

The girls' reunion was cut short by a deafening roar. The unholy worm was gasping its last under the continuing mauling of the crazed wolfman. Its hide was a patchwork of torn and hemorrhaging flesh as it attempted to work its way back to the dark pit from which it had come. But even that short distance of a few yards was too far under the feverish onslaught of its foe's claws. It shuddered violently, let loose a final bellow and then was still. For a few seconds, Cartier continued to tear at its body as if unaware it had stopped moving. When that realization at last penetrated his now animal mentality, he howled in triumph, raising up his blood-soaked claws.

Fury and Wilkerson stood transfixed watching him. Seeing the look of confusion on her friend's face, Fury touched her arm reassuringly. "It's okay. He won't hurt us."

At that, the wolfman snapped his shaggy head around to look at them. Fury reached under her shirt and clasped her medallion. Softly she whispered an incantation of her own. The werewolf growled at the two women, then bolted past them for the main tunnel without a second glance. It was clear he was racing for the exit and the cool freedom of the woods beyond.

"But what will happen to him?" Wilkerson asked with genuine concern.

"He will manage. Trust me, we've done this before. Now we've got to get you back to town and a doctor's care."

"Sounds good to me, but I think I'm going to need your shoulder to lean on for a while."

Seeing that her friend was near complete physical exhaustion, Fury was only too eager to comply. "You do that, Ann. Now, let's get out of this hell hole."

After covering Prof. Wilkerson with her discarded cloak, Fury helped her to the mouth of the cave and the fresh night air. For the next forty minutes, with the professor's left arm draped around her shoulders, she carefully guided them back to Cherryfield.

During their slow hike, Wilkerson filled in the details for Fury. She explained how several of the men from town had discovered the cave during an extended hunting trip. Thinking the cave harmless, they had gone into its depths exploring. Their presence awoke the sleeping other-world entity that was Yog Yoteth. Wilkerson alluded to an origin older than recorded history.

With his ability to infect humans with a single bite of his suckered tentacles, the dark-dwelling aberration used his first slaves to lure others into its clutches. One of these was Sheriff Claymore, who, by his position in the community, quickly became Yoteth's primary agent.

Satisfied that his insidious hold on the small town was firm, the alien god began quenching its taste for blood by directing its twisted followers to seek out sacrificial victims. Thus began the mysterious disappearances that first attracted Dr. Wilkerson's attention.

"I take you weren't fooled by the daily doping the town's folks were subjected to?" Fury surmised, as they shuffled up the center of the still sleeping hamlet.

"No. But only by luck. The first meal I had was in the hotel restaurant, my first night here. One of the waitresses spilled a drink while serving people at the table next to mine. Before she could mop it up, a house cat came over and licked it up.

"While waiting for my meal to arrive, I watched that cat go over to a corner and fall into a stupor within minutes of drinking the spilled water. I decided not to drink anything until I saw what was going on.

"You can deduce the rest."

Fury got Wilkerson back to the hotel just mentioned. The slumbering people were just as they had been hours earlier. She wondered how long the actual drug lasted and natural sleep took over.

"I think we'd best get you showered up and in bed," she told the weary teacher. "First thing tomorrow, I'll find my friend and we'll wrap things up at the cave."

Fury's plan was to procure dynamite from the hardware store and blow up the entrance to the cave.

"But where will you find him?"

"I saw a little church over on the next street, when we first rode into town."

"Yes. What of it?"

"Part of my friend's condition requires him to seek hollowed ground to return to his human guise. It's like some inborn radar that penetrates his wolf mentality and pulls him back."

Wilkerson shook her head slightly. "Kate, you have the strangest friends in the world."

"Isn't that the truth." They started laughing together as they entered the hotel's front door.

The new day's sun was barely cresting the town roofs when Fury drove the Cord up to the white picket fence surrounding the small church. Several hardy citizens were up and about. Not an unusual sight for a rural village like Cheeryfield. Common sense folks didn't waste daylight. She mused at how they would take the news of the night's activities when she eventually filed her report with the state police. Cherryfield would have one hell of a tale to tell.

To the left of the church was a small, very neatly kept cemetery. Fury grabbed a robe from the empty seat and left the car. She went over to the quiet plot where the angels slept and scanned it. Overhead, in a thick oak, a blue jay was screeching his morning hellos.

Cartier, nude, except for what remained of his torn pants, was seated against a cracked tombstone, his back to her.

"It's about time you got here, *mon cheri*."

"I had to get Ann to the doctor's office."

Cartier stood and she did her best not to grin. Donat Cartier was a religious man and awaking half naked on church property was always embarrassing. To say the least. She tossed him the robe.

"*Merci*."

"You're welcome."

"What now?" He pulled on the robe and stepped over the fence.

She looked into his deep, whimsical green eyes and said,

"Now, we go blow things up."

THE END

AIRSHIP 27 TAKES FLIGHT

by Ron Fortier

I've never been good with dates or numbers, just not the way my brain works. But what life has taught me in the past 68 years is nothing happens in a vacuum. No single incident in one's life is ever an isolated event without connections to other events. You see, everything we do is going to have effects on what comes later and the birth of Airship 27 Productions is such a history. It is about multiple events that, when placed in a chronological order, tell that history and all its related consequences. The one irrefutable fact is that this book, "The Hounds of Hell," by yours truly and Gordon Linzner was the first book ever produced by the Airship 27 team although it would not brandish its familiar logo until later editions. So let's go back in time and share this story rife with ups and downs, triumphs and woes.

I was discharged from the U.S. Army in 1968 and came home to Somersworth, NH, to restart my civilian life. Part of that life was being an avid comicbook reader and collector. Somewhere in my high school years I'd gotten the idea that I wanted to be a comicbook writer and once out of the service, I began the process that would eventually get me to that cherished goal. One of the tools to help me with that dream was the weekly newspaper, The Comic Buyer's Guide published by Don & Maggie Thompson. In it were the latest news stories on what the various comic companies were doing etc. At the back of each issue were the personal ads where people advertised and sold their own amateur publications. What we called fanzines. Intrigued by these, I was soon ordering lots of them and eventually began writing for some. Fanzines were the testing grounds for many of the writers and artists who later went on to become well known professionals in the industry.

I started out buying comic fanzine but along the way my interests were piqued by two other related zines, one that dealt with the world of the old pulp heroes and the other was a digest sized fiction-zine called "Space & Time." Robert Weinberg was a pulp lover – historian who spent the majority of his professional life preserving classic pulp magazines and heroes. At this time he was reprinted small facsimile booklets reprinting tales of long forgotten pulp heroes and villains. They sold for $5 each and after buying one, I was hooked and continued to purchase every new title he would put out. Meanwhile I was also enjoying "Space & Time" published by New

Yorker Gordon Linzner. It was usually filled with terrific short horror, fantasy or science fiction tales. I bought a yearly subscription to it and ultimately began submitting stories. Much to delight, Gordon accepted several of them and just like that my writing career was becoming a reality.

It seems natural to me looking back on all this that sooner or later I would bring these two new loves together and it happened like this. One month Weinberg's pulp reprint book featured four stories starring one of the goofiest pulp heroes of them all; the Moon Man. Det. Steve Thatcher, of Great City, was a modern day Robin Hood who hated the fact that the rich of his city lived without a care in the world while the majority of hard working folks were struggling through the Great Depression. Unable to allow this disparity to continue, Thatcher became a masked vigilante who robbed from the rich and then saw the money distributed to the poor by two of his cohorts. What was truly weird was that his disguise was not your regular domino style mask or hood; it was a fish bowl. You see Thatcher had somehow gotten ahold of a globe made of one way Argus glass. It opened in two sections, was fitted over his head and then snapped together. With the globe over his head, Thatcher could see out, but Argus glass' mirror-like surface prevented anyone from seeing in. Thus, when he was moving through a darkened room while committing his burglaries, all that was visible to any witness was a shiny globe floating along; thus the name given him by the newspapers and police, the Moon Man. The creator-writer of this extremely popular character was Frederic C. Davis.

The very next month Weinberg's booklet featured a dastardly pulp villain named Doctor Satan who appeared in the pages of Weird Tales, arguably the most famous of all the pulp magazines. Created by Paul Ernst, Doctor Satan was a bizarre criminal mastermind who used both science and magic to commit his horrendous crimes. He wore an all read costume and a horned cowl of the same blood hue. Of course you can't have a bad guy without his nemesis, the stalwart hero. In this series he was Criminologist Ascott Keane, who, like Satan, was a master both of science and the occult. They battled each other in a half dozen adventures of which Weinberg had collected four. I devoured them all.

It was a short while later that the idea of a crossover story came to me. Crossovers were something I'd learned while reading Marvel and DC comics as a boy. It basically meant two heroes from different titles would come together in one tale. Fans loved these team-ups and they happened quite often in comics. Which was what got me thinking, why not the pulps? To the best of my then limited pulp knowledge, no one had ever done a pulp actioner where the characters from two different series came together. What if the insidious Doctor Satan and his minions came to Great City to hatch their latest crime? Obviously Ascott Keane would follow them there. So, what would happen if, in chasing Satan, Keane crossed paths with the Moon Man? The more the idea evolved, the more I knew it was something worthwhile that would be fun to write. But I was still unsure of my skills as a writer and decided to seek some assistance in getting this concept down on paper. I contacted Gordon Lizner and asked him if he would help me write such a crossover pulp adventure. To my delight, he agreed but on the condition that I write up the plot and educate him on who these characters were. I was only too happy to comply with his wishes and within a few days sent him a detailed outline to what would become "The Hounds of Hell."

I should mention that Gordon did warn me, even as we were writing it, that most likely there was no market for such a story and it would probably never see print. He came very close to being right about that. I think it only took us a little over a month to write what was basically a novella. Both of us kept copies and it was always agreed I would be the person responsible for finding a home for it. It didn't take me all that long to learn his prophecy that nobody would want such an oddball story soon became true and after almost a year of rejections, I filed it away resigned to the fact that it would never see print.

Now keep in mind, while all this was going on, there were lots of other things happening in my life, the most notable was eventually getting a comic script published and becoming a bonafide professional writer. Part of this came about because of my friendship with Hawaiian artist Gary Kato who I had met through his work in various fanzines. We became a team, and when Gary was recruited by Mike Friedrich of the Star Reach Agency this led to my getting a similar call. After signing with Mike, he urged me to come to California and attend the San Diego Comic Con. My wife Valerie and I did this both in 1989 and 1990. From those trips came my gigs writing the Green Hornet and Terminator comic series for Now Comics. Time was moving along. Our children were becoming young adults, I kept punching that clock at the GE factory where I maintained my "day" job while continuing to get more writing gigs.

Meanwhile artist Rob Davis had gotten his own career steamrolling first with jobs at Malibu Comics and Innovation until at last getting assignments for DC doing their Star Trek comics. Somewhere in all these years, I wrote Rob a fan letter, having become a fan of his work on a series called "Scimidar." From that pre-internet correspondence we built a true friendship and made several attempts to sell proposals to DC. None of them hit a bullseye and by the time personal computers were the norm, we'd drifted apart. The comicbook boom of the 80s died out rather quickly and many of the smaller houses disappeared putting lots of creators out of work. Rob left the comic business for a job driving a bus in Missouri. After Now Comics went under, I kept busy write for small independent outfits and hooked up with a group of creators from Maine calling themselves Alpha Productions.

One of the Alpha writers was Chris Mills. After a few years of making comics with Alpha, Chris landed an editorial job with a new outfit out of Florida called Tekno Comics. Tekno was owned by a husband and wife team who had absolutely no idea of how to run a comic company. Several months after settling into his new editorial position, Chris contacted me asking if I would be willing to write for Tekno. He explained that the company was horribly mismanaged and he didn't think it would last more than a few years. But they were throwing obscene amounts of money at their creators and I'd be smart to sign on. Now my mother did not raise any addle brained children. If somebody wanted to throw money my way, I was all to ready to catch as much of it as possible. I told Chris to throw my hat in the Tekno ring. A few days later I received a call from a fellow named James Chambers.

Jim Chambers was another editor at Tekno Comics who had been assigned a science fiction series based on an unused TV pilot by the late Star Trek guru, Gene Roddenberry. The comic was called, "Gene Roddenberry's Lost Universe" and at that time it was being written by a popular sci-fi writer who had no clue how to write comics. Jim and I hit it off immediately and over the phone I told him how I'd go about writing the book if I were given assignment. He liked my ideas a great deal and I was hired to take over the book. As memory serves, I wrote "Lost Universe" for almost a year before Tekno ultimately exploded, as Chris had predicted. It came as no surprise. It had been an interesting experience for two very positive factors; one I made lots of money and two, I became good friends with Jim Chambers.

With Tekno now comics history, Jim returned to his home in New York state, got another job and restarted his own career as a writer of horror and fantasy. Several months later he contacted me via e-mail to tell me a fellow named Vincent Sneed was putting together an anthology to feature women as the heroes and I might want to consider contributing a story to it. I contacted Sneed and learned he wanted a good mix of genres for his book and would be happy if I submitted a "pulp" tale. I sat down and created a female heroine called Kate Fury and wrote her one and only adventure, "Fury in Vermont." Sneed liked it a great deal and published it in his "Dark Furies" anthology. I was thrilled and began to wonder if he might not be the fellow to look at "The Hounds of Hell" after all these years. I mentioned it to him. He said it didn't sound like his cup of tea.... BUT....he knew a guy who was deeply into reprinting classic pulp stories and I should contact him. That person was Ron Hanna of Wild Cat Books.

Now Hanna was a true-blue pulp fan and had been producing pulp reprint books for a nearly ten years at this time. I managed to find some of these on-line (yes, the internet had been born by then and the world was getting connected fast).

Meanwhile Chris Mills had started a website and asked me to write a series of pulp short stories starring a zombie-like avenger. Mills wanted this character to be in the vein of the Shadow and the Spider and had come up with a name...and nothing else. That is important because later things went sour for various reasons, which I'll get to shortly. All you need to know is that in a period of two years, I wrote six tales of this Undead Avenger that were all posted on his website. At one point, Mills ran an art contest looking for the best depiction of the Undead Avenger. Among those sending in entries were artists Tom Floyd and Rob Davis, both of whom had gotten into the comic game years earlier via the same small Texas independent comic company. Floyd won the contest with a gorgeous oil painting, while Rob's was a close second.

This is also where I should tell you that I had, again thanks to the internet, reconnected with Rob Davis and from that re-acquaintance emerged our first ever project together, the graphic novel, "Daughter of Dracula." All of this was happening at the same time I was discovering Ron Hanna and Wild Cat Books. Taking Vincent Sneed's advice, I wrote to Hanna and told him about my novella in which the Moon Man battled Doctor Satan and asked if he'd be interested in reading it? When he replied affirmatively, I dug into my files, found that old manuscript and mailed it off with all fingers crossed.

I don't think anyone was more surprised than yours truly when Hanna accepted the book for publication. At which point I made it clear that I wanted control over the design of the book. I'd seen enough of Hanna's previous titles and though fun, they were amateurish. If "The Hounds of Hell" was finally going to be published, I wanted to make sure it was a professional package from the first page to the last. I asked Rob if he would be willing to do several interior illustrations to go along with the story and he gladly agreed. Then, having been so impressed with Tom Floyd's painting of my Undead Avenger, I hit him up to do a wrap-around cover for the book. Tom delivered beyond our wildest dreams, splitting his dramatic image so that the principle players, the Moon Man and Doctor Satan appear on the front cover and when you turn it over, there are Ascott Keane and his girl Friday, Beatrice Dale, about to be cut in half by Satan's laser beam. It's pure pulp all the way. Having admired Vincent Sneed's design work on "Dark Furies," I recruited him to do the design logo and he turned in an eye-catching design that totally enhanced Floyd's painting.

Being a novella, I realized the book would be on the skimpy side and so suggested to Hanna that we add two of my short stories, "Lady Arcane, Mistress of Magic" and "Angel In His Sights." Both featured a single illustration. There was also a bio page for all the creators involved with the title and more ads for previous Wild Cat Books. Hanna wrote a very nice introduction and in the back we had an ad for our next project; a book collecting the six pulp tales of the Undead Avenger character I'd created for that website mentioned earlier. Floyd had agreed to let us use his amazing painting for the cover and Sneed again took on the role of designer. It would be our second book for Wild Cat Books. Within a year of all this, I asked for ownership of this grim character…and to my disappointment, was refused. In the end, Rob and I merely changed the character's name, and the names of the supporting characters and setting, reprinted his stories (which were rightfully mine from day one). I continue to chronicle his adventures to this day. Fans know him as Brother Bones.

The only thing left for me to do was notify Gordon Linzner, my co-writer that, after almost ten years, I had done the impossible after all and gotten somebody to publish our new pulp adventure. Linzner was both surprised and delighted. He's a great guy and I owe him so much.

Thus "The Hounds of Hell," by Ron Fortier and Gordon Linzner, debut in 2005 from Wild Cat Books. And that was the start of what would become Airship 27 Productions, though that brand and logo were still a few titles away. In time, Rob, as official Art Director, would design our dirigible logo and we would do a few books with New York based designed Anthony Schiavino. We soon parted company with Wild Cat Books to go our own course.

Today Airship 27 Productions is one of the leading publishers in the New Pulp field and we have over a hundred titles in our catalogs that range from every pulp genre you can shoot a .45 caliber slug at. And in that process, we've won a few awards, launched a few writing and art careers and helped make New Pulp an honest-to-goodness movement that has been a totally positive influence on keeping pulp fandom alive and well.

Of course nothing in life is ever 100% smooth and carefree and Airship 27's birth had its share of bumps along the road. As I've said, part of this journey meant working with people for a short while and then moving on to whatever our next plateau was. We did our best to contact ourselves honorably at every step of the way but sometimes others didn't view things in the same perspective. I'm all too aware there are folks out there who will find many faults with this little history I've put forth. That is their right and we certainly do not begrudge them for it. We never set out to compete with anyone but ourselves.

In the end, with God's blessings, Airship 27 Productions exists and for the most part I'd like to think that makes lots and lots of people very happy. And with the Creator's continual blessings, we plan on being around for a long time to come.

Thanks for reading and always for your continued support. We couldn't have done any of this without each and every one of you Loyal Airmen.

Ron Fortier
5/24/2015
Fort Collins, CO